I0748498

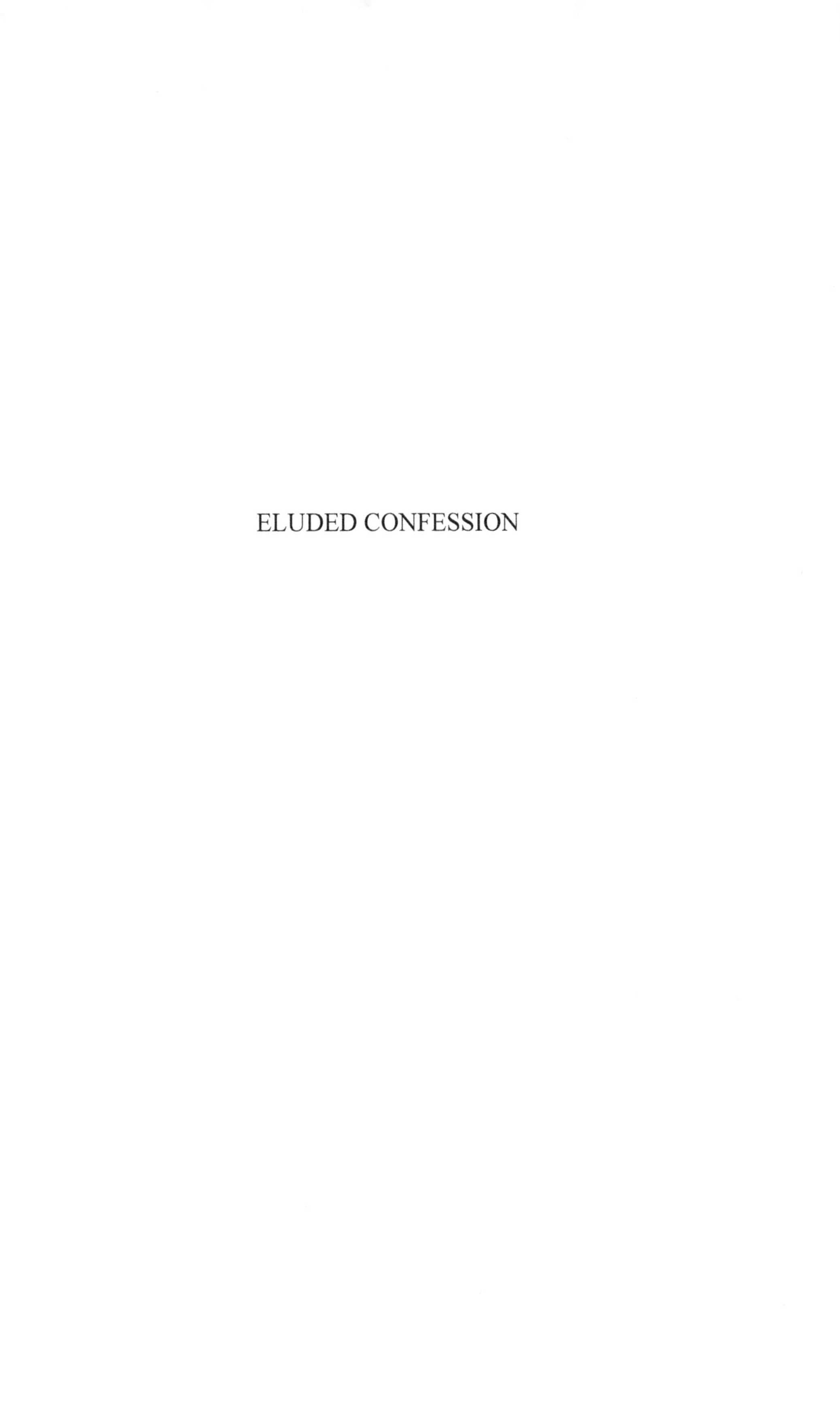

ELUDED CONFESSION

Warning — Disclaimer

Every effort has been made to make this Novel of Fiction complete and accurate as possible. However, there may be mistakes, both typographical and in it's contents. Therefore, this text should not be used as a general guide. The purpose of this Novel is to Entertain. The author and the Publishing company shall have neither liability nor responsibility to any person or entity with respect to any one person or group of persons, any loss or damage caused, or alleged to have been caused, directly or indirectly, by the information contained in this book. By purchasing this book you are bound by the above.

ELUDED CONFESSION

BY
MICHAEL J. STUCKEY JR.

Stuckey Publishing

Stuckey Publishing
USA
www.ardentwriter.com

Second Edition 2017
Print ISBN: 978-0-9986715-0-5
eBook ISBN: 978-0-9986-715-1-2

Previously Published
by, SBPRA; 2016
ISBN# 978-1-68181-379-0

About the Author

As a child Michael began writing. He said, "I've had the opportunity to travel and see many parts of the world. I've partaken and indulged within the pleasures, in the pain and suffering of romance. Every to do urge, morally wrong or right, bad judgment, sexual fantasy, impulse and desire I've fulfilled. I have flat lined four times, fell in love once, and I can't wait to do it all again!"

Try; you may, though unable to forget, unable to look away. Her fate: a written calamity, exposing your longing, your inner-most secret desires, beckoning your unease. For your dismay, her legacy is of your infliction.

Contents

1
CHOSEN

Fourteen months ago

Through the window. She's amazing. Long, brown straight hair with a purple streak, hanging down the left side of her face. High cheekbones, with black eyeliner. Bare; full lips. Tight jaw line. Draped around her thin neck is a chain choker. She has no shirt on and no bra on. She turns ever so slightly to her right, towards me. Her breasts, they're perfectly shaped, as big as melons. They're perky, firm, and close together. My God, they're perfect.

She stands up from her bed, flat toned stomach. Walks into her bathroom. She's only five foot three inches, maybe five foot five inches tall with toned arms, and her fingernails are painted black. She is wearing black lace panties, barely covering a toned, tight, undercut apple-bottom shaped ass. She leans over the sink, filling her glass with water. Wow. Her panties outline the crack of her ass, down into the bottom outline of her ass cheeks, the inside of her toned thighs, how the thighs and her ass join at the beginning of her taint, running down to the plush thick lips of her Cooch. She has well defined legs down to her thin ankles and black painted toenails. She's walking back into the room with a glass of water, a towel, and a really beautifulathame. Her skin looks flawless except for her upper right, top inside thigh where there are several scars of self inflicted cuts.

She sits down in a chair, between the corner of her dresser and the bathroom door. She snaps the towel open, lifting her right leg and lays it underneath her thigh. I back away from the window and walk around the back of the house. The second window in from the left is open, as I climb through the window into the living room, I hear the radio. It's playing, Nickel-back "Love to Hate You." Slowly I walk through the house. I pull a black S & M mask out of my back-right pocket, lift it up above my head, and pull it down over my face. The mask has three zippers, one for each eye enabling me to see, and one for my mouth, allowing me to taste.

I pull a length of rope out of my left back pocket and continue walking through the house. I see recent pictures of her parents. She must be about seventeen or eighteen years old. I step in to the bedroom doorway and stare at her. She is cutting her inside thigh, slicing from the middle of the inside right thigh, slowly dragging the blade into the skin, pulling up to the top of her thigh. She looks up, rolling her eyes back, exhaling with relief.

As she lowers her head back down, she sees me, screams; she jumps up from the chair and throws a glass of water at me. I speed walk up to her. She's swinging with her right hand, trying to cut me with her athame. As she lunged forward to jab me with the knife, I grab her hand, pull her to my right and step left behind her. I twist her hand forward and pull down, back and up toward the center of her back. With my left arm, I reached around the front of her. Across her left arm and further across her mid-drift 'n' wrestle her face down on the hardwood floor of her bedroom. I straddle over her, sitting on her upper legs at the bottom of her rump, pulling her arms behind her back. I tie her wrists together and stand up.

She rolls on to her back, pinning her arms beneath her against the floor. She's screaming and cussing at me, trying to kick me. I back-step and just stare. Slowly, I pull my black leather gloves off, finger by finger, removing each glove. I reach to the right and lay the leather gloves on her dresser. I step to the right and take two steps forward. Now, standing parallel to her mid-drift, I lean down, grabbing her arms just below her shoulders, on her biceps. I squeeze as I lift her straight up, her feet dangling in the air. I turn to my left, towards the bed, take a step in, and toss her back away from me. She lands on the bed and bounces a little. With my head slightly tilted, I stare.

She's lying on the bed, as she was on the floor. She is still trying to kick me and has yet to stop screaming 'n' cursing me out. Softly I began grazing my fingers over her body, from her knees, up her outer thigh, over the front of her hip and across her abs, up gently, cupping her left breast, squeezing ever so softly. A moment goes by, and I open my hand, releasing her tit. I slide my hand between her breast up to her neck and begin to squeeze, just for a second. Then I slide my hand back down to her stomach.

She is panicking, crying, shaking, and wiggling around, trying to get away, as one could not help but to fight. With my right hand, I pulled out an eight inch long knife from my belt sheath. She's becoming hysterical. Slowly, section by section, I cut away her panties, her tight black lace panties, from her skin. She tries to pull her legs together, to cross them, but I am kneeling over her left leg. I continued, cutting and peeling away each strip, until she is completely naked. I drag the knife over her body, to let her feel the cold of the steel.

I take a hold of her neck, just below her jaw, with my left hand, to hold her head still, as I taste her lips. She tries to pull her face, her lips away. In return, I begin to punish her. Gently I be- gin sliding the knife edge of the blade up her stomach, between her breasts, dragging the tip up over the top of her left breast and back down to the bottom. I begin making a shallow, short cut on the bottom of her breast, ever so slow and lightly, to leave no permanent scars. All the while, I never say a word, not even a peep or grunt. I slice the top layer of skin, allowing her to feel the serenity, the burning sting as the edge of the blade pierces and separates her skin. Just a drip. Then the entire cut becomes swollen and has a growing trickle of blood emerging. I lay my lips on her left breast, over the cuts. I open my mouth a little more. With my tongue, I lick the blood, cleaning off her lovely breast, while I massage her Tit from over top and down to the nipple, ever so lightly squeezing and pinching her nipple, suckling, until the bleeding of her perfect breast has stopped. I get up off her, as she tries to kick me, yet again.

I catch her legs and spin her around. I pull her left leg, raising her ankle in front of her and up to her head. I reach over to the nightstand and pull the cloth dowel off the lampshade. I rip it into one long strip and bind her left ankle with the one end. With the other end, I wrap the cloth around her thin neck. Not too tight, just tight enough for erotic asphyxiation. I turn her a little more and kneel down at the side of the bed. Raise her right leg up and over my left shoulder. As she tries to kick me with her right ankle, I drag the edge of my Athame over the outer lips of her pussy, then, with the back edge of the blade, I pull down between, separating her swollen pink, purplish lips, and begin to lick. I lay the knife down and indulge in eating her out. Occasionally, I pull her left leg just a little, then release to encourage the restriction of air and intensify her orgasm. Her perineum is intact. I slowly puncture through, inserting my pointer between her lips, and she comes. She taste unbelievably sweet. As she bleeds, I slide my fingers up inside her vagina and my pinky into her ass. I continue eating, licking her clitoris, while sliding my pointer inside from side to top, to side, in and out, slow to rough, fast to slow, as she couldn't take anymore, with her thighs buckling and her body twitching, her internal muscles throbbing. I lightly cut across her lips just above her clitoris. Blood emerges and begins to drip down. She starts to come, mixing with the blood running down her lips. I drink in, drink, and absorb her endorphins, her come, sending me into an insatiable rage of lust.

I stand up, lower my pants to my calves, untie her left leg and I climb on the bed straddling over her mid-drift. I lay my rod between her amazing breast, move my hands over taking a hold of the out sides of her rack, and with my hands, I begin moving her yaya's up and down, jerking myself off with her perfect melons. I come on her face, and I come on her neck. I slap her cheek with my spitting stick. Relieved, however; far from satisfied, I slide my left leg back, over and off the right side of the bed as my body spins away from her. I stand up, turn back to her, raise up and retie her left ankle to the cloth around her neck. I grab her by her right leg, and lift straight up. I look down amazed at the view of her. With my pants sliding down around my ankles and a painfully throbbing hard-on that won't quit. I lean in, reach over with a firm grip of her right leg, spin her pa-dunk-a-dunk towards me, dragging her ass to the edge of the bed.

***

Yesterday

All the townspeople congregated at the Small town courthouse, waiting for him to be sentenced.

The jury comes back in.

The Judge asked the jury foreperson, "How do you find the Defendant?"

"We, the jury, find Sargent; David Campbell guilty of first-degree murder, on each count of the thirteen families he brutally murdered. For a total of thirty-one people."

"On the charges of kidnapping, raping, torturing, and cannibalistic activities of one Marriessa, of the age nineteen. How do you find?"

"We, the jury, find one Sargent; David Campbell, guilty!"

"On the charges of unlawful restraint, mutilation resulting in the murder of our beloved Lieutenant; William Graham, how do you find?"

"We, the jury, find one Sargent; David Campbell guilty on all counts!"

"Jury foreperson, members of the jury, you are excused. Thank you for your diligence of service on these court proceedings. Sargent; David Campbell, will you please rise. You have been found guilty on all charges and all counts. Is there anything you'd like to say before I pass judgment and sentence you?"

Sargent; David Campbell says, "Your Honor, I did not, nor could I have done such heinous acts. You know me, Billy. We grew up together. Please, please?"

"I heard enough. I am sentencing you, David Campbell, previously a Sargent in this great town of Toulon, Illinois, to death. You will be imprisoned for the time it takes the henchman to prepare. You will be executed for your heinous acts. Execution will be death by electrocution. May you be denied the shelter of our good Lord and Savior, so that you suffer. May you have a glimpse of the pain that you have caused to the families of our great town and of your victims."

***

Later that Night in a Bar

"The Night was Drawn and Gloomy. This Drifter was strangely upbeat. He was driving a Hunter green 2006 Dodge Ram 1500Pickup with an eight foot bed, a standard factory package with standard tires. The Drifter drives up and parks at Kasey Jones Pub & Grub, the local Police Bar in Chat-tum, Missouri. The drifter got out of his Dodge Pickup wearing black single strap biker boots, blue jeans, and a white T-shirt underneath a denim button up shirt. The four top buttons were undone, and his shirts were neatly tucked in to his pants. (The Look of James Dean.) He even had a wallet with a belt chain. The chain was not a chain,not at all. It was a blade from a chain saw.

"He walks into the Bar (Pausing) as he glances around the room, noticing, on the left, five on-duty, Small Town Cops. They get quiet and stare at the stranger as he walks in, so he looks to the right and sees a square clock with antlers wrapped around as a frame. It reads nine pm Wednesday. As he strolls up to the bar, he notices pictures of southern rock singers, beer signs, a pool table, and a few table chairs. To the back right of the Bar is the bathroom.

"The Barkeep in his black jeans & greasy ripped up T-shirt says, 'What will it be?'

"The Drifter replies, 'Tall and Cold. Whatever is on Tap.'

"The Barkeep brings a twenty-four ounce mug of whatever is on tap, a no-name, bland beer no one ever heard of and says, 'So where you in from?'

"'I've been Here, I've been there, never been home.'

"The Barkeep says, 'I'm Alex and You are?' With his hand out, as if to shake.

"With an empty pausing stare, the drifter replies, 'My name, is Gavin Michael,' as he reaches over to shake Alex's hand.

"'A firm grip. I Like that,' Gavin said and continued on to say, 'Been driving a day and a week. I could use a room.'

"He pauses and glances back at the cops, realizing they're all sitting at a round table drinking Beer and Shots. The Small Town Cops appear to be paying attention to him. Gavin boasting loudly says, 'Alex. Hey Alex, I've got a story that will floor you.'

"'Well, Gavin, nothing else to do. Here's the key. Let's hear it.' (As the Cops gossip and make snide remarks amongst themselves.)

"'Where do I start,' says Gavin. 'Okay. Well. It all started six years ago today back in the Mountains of Connecticut, Rattle Snake Mountain to be specific. There was this guy, nothing special, averaged height, build, average looks, just his eyes. His eyes were empty as if he had no soul. He had the dirtiest, shitty, rust bucket of a Pickup Truck that I ever did see. Glue, spit, dirt, and duct tape seemed to be holding this truck together.

"Laughing, Alex tries to say, 'That sounds like my piece of shit truck.'

"Gavin goes on to say, 'I don't know his name but for story sake I'll call him Angellous. So Angellous is loading his truck with what looked like an assortment of knives, an Athame on his hip, and a 30-06 Rifle, a 45 caliber Smith & Wesson Pistol. As he walks back into the house, I notice Angellous is covered in blood. An hour or two goes by, he's finally coming out of the house. Angellous is smiling, walking out to the truck. Wearing tan construction boots, blue jeans, a black T-shirt, and a 1980's denim jacket and gloves. I wait as Angellous drives away. Half hour goes by I walk up to the house. Blood, so much blood, blood everywhere, like someone uncontrollably barfed or sprayed it all over. It's everywhere man. The couch, the end tables, walls, even the floor appears to be painted with blood, except a few blotches where you can see it has wooden floor boards.

"A young boy, who can't be more than fifteen or sixteen years old, is nailed to the wall. His back is all cut up and partly skinned. The skin that was removed was stretched out and stapled to the floor. Etched on the back of the kid's neck, it looked like a mark, a mark of a 3 and something. I turn and look around the room, adjacent to the body, above the TV, and say to myself, 'What is that, drawn in blood?' So I continue to look through the rest of the house."

"Alex asks, 'What the hell is it?'

"Gavin says, 'A symbol.'

"'Symbol of what?'

"'Here I'll draw it for you.'

Gavin starts again with the story.

"I walked down the hallway to what appeared to be, what was once a kitchen. There are no floors, only rafters, broke-down cabinets, some with no doors, some doors barely hanging on. Dishes, I think, piled up in the sink. Mold covered food on the counters, and table with shell casings and what I guess is a bullet press. I see a stairwell in the back left corner of the kitchen, so I move across the rafters to get to the stairs and I go up.

"There's bloody smudges, scrapes, and hand-prints going up the stairs. I come to a door. As I open the door, a girl's body falls to the floor. She must have been propped against the door. She is stripped naked. There are bruises on her arms as if she was held down and ligature marks on her neck, black and blues on the back of her thighs and on her back. I squat down to see if she's alive. Her wrists are cut. I check for a pulse on her neck. Blood. Her throat is cut. Her heart beats no more. She looks like she was washed clean. Her body showed burns and marks as if she was tortured, and, not much unlike the boy, a symbol is carved into the skin on the back of her neck.

"So I walked out of the room back into the hallway and look to my right. I walk on down to the only other door. I see that the door is open, I hesitate. I ask out loud, 'What monstrosity will I find in here?' The room is immaculate with pictures of the kids and an older lady. Thankfully she's not here. Military dressed bed, neatly folded clothes. Appalled and yet at contentment, I walk back out to my truck and go to the Local Sheriff's Station.

***

"It's just about nightfall. I walk into the Sheriff's Station. There is only one Police Officer there. He is about five foot five inches and looks to be about two-hundred and sixty pounds of a slow, snaggle-tooth, fat bastard. Surprisingly, he appears clean. I say, 'Sheriff, I'd like to report a double murder.'

"Sheriff says, 'Whoa, Whoa, simmer down.'

"I notice the chest badge says, 'Sheriff D. Little'

"Sheriff Little goes on to say, 'Now what's your malfunction, boy?'

"'They're dead, They're all dead and he's gone.'

"'Who's Dead? Who's Gone? Just calm down. Tell me what you did.'

"'No, not me. This guy I saw, this guy leaving a house covered in blood. I waited about an hour. then went in the house, horrible. What he did to those kids.'

"'Where's this House?'

"'The old dirt road up the back of Rattle Snake Mountain. Third drive on left.'

"'Wait here. You best be fix'in to stay. I'm gonna check this out.'

"He's driving a red shitty ford pickup, Sheriff!"

So the Sheriff leaves.

"A few moments later, I leave as well. I jump back in my truck and head on down the Interstate. I'm a truck-in, pushing tin. Easy rock listening 101.1fm, south bound Rt.84 with a big foot pedal slammed to the floor. 'What is it I see? Is it? It can't be. It is.' It's the red shitty rust-bucket Ford. It's him. So I cut back five or six car lengths and follow him.

"I hear on the radio:

"'Just in: a man wanted for questioning in a gruesome double murder. If you have any information on whereabouts of a green, Dodge Ram Pickup, do not approach. Call your local Sheriff. Believed to be armed and dangerous. Repeat. Do not approach! Wanted for questioning. Any information on the location of this vehicle and its driver should be reported to your local Sheriff.'

"I truck on down. I see a rest stop and I pull on in. It's an old-style truck stop. Has a diner called: The Grease Pit. There's a few gas pumps off to the back left of the Diner. Big rig trucks everywhere else in the parking lot. I parked off to the right, facing the Diner. I watched him go in, sit-down and like an arrogant sun of a bitch, he ordered. Several minutes go by, I'm too far away to see what he is eating. It looks like a sandwich. It must be good. He is wolfing it down like he hasn't eaten in days. He gets up and disappears into the back of the diner for about fifteen minutes. He comes back to the table and throws money on the table. Then he walks back out to his truck. It's now morning. He pulls around to the gas pump, so I pull up to the pumps as well. As I start pumping my gas, I hear:

"'What a long road, this life we lead!'

"I turn. It's Angellous, so I reply, 'I suppose it is. My name is Gavin.'

"Angellous has a confused look on his face and says, 'This been fun; however, I have lessons to teach. I bid you good day, my friend.'

"Then Angellous turns away, unhooks the pump nozzle. He jumps in the truck, starts up the shitty rust bucket, and pulls off. So I top off and follow him. We stopped a few more times for gas. During the last stop, now night, we talked.

"Angellous says, 'Gavin is it?'

"I replied, 'Yes.'

"'You got a problem or some-thin, Gavin?'

"'No. No problem.'

"'What's your 20?'

"'Arizona. I'll take a detour there. A good Woman, though a few days with her, a few too many. If you know what I mean.'

"Pumps click, we hang up the nozzles and nod to each other as we pull off. Pass each other a few more times, like playing tag. Come up to an exit for NY State Park, NY. I pull off for some shuteye. I drive into the Park, find a nice place to spend the night. Well, what's left of it. Pull out my roll bag and walk on up to the rocks, find a place to lay. A few hours and the warmth of the sun on my face wakes me up. I roll up my bag, stroll back to the truck. I see Angellous as I load my bag in behind the back seat.

"Angellous says, 'Breakfast?' Hands me jerky.

"'Thank you,' I said.

"'Some view.'

"'Yes, but must get on. Good talk-in,' I say as I climb back in my truck.

"'Gavin, I think I'll join you, if you don't mind. I have a few stops I have to make along the way though.'

"'Ya, company would be good.'As I pull off, I say to myself, 'Fuck me, I'm an Asshole. What I get my self into.' So I follow him.

2
DIRTY SLAP

"We stop off in Flemington, Pennsylvania. We pull up to this house: Fifteen Mocking Bird Lane. It is midday Friday. I can see a little, blue ranch-style house, with a horseshoe driveway. Woods to the left. To the right in back it looks like a hedgerow of trees and shrubs, then opens into a field.

"Angellous says, 'Get some shuteye. I'll wake you up when my lessons are over.'

"I reply, 'All right then.'

"Angellous walks back to the truck, grabs the 30-06 Rifle, then walks into the house as if it was his own, so I run up to the side window.

"I see, Angellous knocks out the woman from behind with the butt of the rifle stock. She's wearing a white laced slip, damn she looks good. She's about five foot, brown hair, nice neckline. They got to be C's. Her stomach is flat. Angellous drags her into the living room, rips out the phone and uses the cord to tie her hands behind her back to her waist. Throws her to the floor, then walks through another door. A moment later he is dragging a man, kicking and screaming. The guy is about six foot four inch- es, and he's dragging him like a rag doll into the living room by the woman. Angellous hits the man with the phone and knocks him out, hog ties him. Puts a gag in his mouth. Angellous sits down on the sofa sharpening his Athame, waiting for what I can only guess is for him to awake.

"The man awakes groaning, grunting. Angellous gets up, cuts the white slip off the woman, and knocks her onto the floor. Hysterical she's becoming. Now on her back, he leans over her and cuts, little cuts at first, on her arms, then on her stomach. He kneels down beside her, reaches to his left, taking hold of her legs by her ankles. He pulls her legs up, then down. Her knees bend as her feet are forced to the sides of her head. With her white slip, he ties the ankles together. He grabs the lady's hair and pulls her head forward as he slid her white slip-bound ankles over her head and down behind her neck.

"He unbuttons his pants and lowers them down around his ass, kneels down, and leans over her, staring in her face. Slowly he slides his hard-on inside her, and enjoys slow and gentle penetration, then eagerly thrusts to vigorous sex. Her pear shaped tits are jarring up and down. Just as he is about to finish, he pulls out, grabs her right outer thigh, and flips her to the left toward the couch, flipping her over. Her ankles are still tied down behind the back of her neck. He lifts her by her hips and ass and he forces himself into her ass. Slamming, bouncing her into himself, her face and chest are getting rug burn.

"He finally stops. With a smile on his face, he glances back over his shoulder at the man and pulls his dick out of her ass. With his left hand, he grabs a hold of his penis at the base and pulls up and off, turns around and leans to the man, and slaps his bloody shit covered hand, right into the man's face. Laughing, he turns back to the lady, leans back over her again, and cuts her ankles loose. He grabs her by her hair, pulling her up in front of the man.

"He picks up the knife and steps around behind her, reaches down over her right shoulder, and stabbing her three times in the chest, between her breasts. He lets go of her hair and yanks the knife out of her chest. She falls to the floor. He walks over, grabs the man by his hair, and drags him to the couch. Unties his wrist. He forces him to write a note. Angellous then leans the man's head forward and etches a symbol in the back of his neck, as the man screams and cries.

"He pulls the guy up by his hair, until he is on his knees, props the butt of the stock of the 30-06 on the floor and shoves the barrel into the guy's mouth, forcing him to push down on the trigger, blowing out the top and back of his skull. Then he walks back to the lady, turns her head, and etches the same thing in the back of her neck. Angellous goes into the bathroom. twenty min- utes go by. He comes out of the bathroom, all cleaned up. I run back to my truck and act like I'm sleeping.

"Angellous knocks on the window, wakes me up and says to me, 'You ready? Got some miles ahead of us.'

"'Ya, Ya, I'm good, I'm up.'

"So off we go down the street, back onto Rt. 84 south bound. A couple of hours go by. We are now on Rt. 284 south.

***

We stop for gas. It's another old-style truck stop (not many left in the states, good food and cheap.) Not much different than the last, except the diner's name is Ray's Grill, just past Harrisburg Pennsylvania. So it's Friday night and we're filling up our tanks off Rt.248.

"Angellous says, 'I have another lesson to teach. It'll take about two or three days.'

"'Alright perhaps I will see you in Arizona.' He didn't say where and I didn't ask.

"'Ya. No – Gavin, why don't you meet me in Toulon, Illinois, end of Draut Rd.'

"'Well, I should be getting going.'

"'What's another two or three days? I got something you gotta see!'

"'Ya, alright, meet you there. Say Monday.'

"'It's a plan. You'll like it!'

"So, gassed up, off I go back on Rt.248 south down to Rt.78 westbound not far from the junction. What a sweet straight run that Rt.480 west will be! I stopped off in Willard, Ohio, just off the road for some shuteye. I awake. It's now Saturday morning, and I head on back toward rt.480. Son of a Bitch. There's the truck, Angellous's truck. I stopped to see what he is doing parked in the driveway of a tan, two-storied, split bi-level house with Spanish clay roof, here in Willard.

"I walk up to the front door and look in the accented window. Empty hall. I look through the living room window and don't see anyone, so I look in the sun-room window on the right side of the house: empty; there is no one. I walk back around the front and knock. The door swings open as I knock. 'HELLO.' I walk in. 'HELLO. Any one home?' No answer, so I look around.

***

Meanwhile, back at Kasey Jones Pub & grub

As Gavin has been telling this story, the small-town cops, still noisy and sarcastic. Ask for his ID, busting his chops, asking about the story.

Now fed up with their bantering, Gavin says to the cops, "Sit down, shut-up. I can't tell you what happens if you keep interrupting and asking stupid questions. Be patient and all will be revealed. Now where was I? Yes, to see what Angellous is doing at a house in Willard. About a mile from where I pulled over for shuteye."

***

Willard

"Nice setup. From the door, a hallway. To my right is an office. To the left, a family-room. Down the hall to the right, a living-room. Nothing special: another hallway. To the left, Holy Shit. A pot rack above the center-Island counter. It's not hanging pots. Nope, there are no pots. There are Arms, calf's, thighs. It looks like a Meat Locker. 'Wait. What's that sizzling?' A slab of meat with a Tattoo. Next to the frying skillet, a boiling pot I dipped a ladle into the pot and scoop out, Boiled Brain. It resembles worms. As I turn to go out the kitchen sliding door, onto the deck, trying not to puke, I stop. I see Angellous washing knives with the water hose. I back up away from the door and I creep through the house to head back out the front door.

"As I am walking out, I think, let me warn the neighbors. I walk off the front porch, walk to my right (the left of the house) stop, and look around the side of the house, so he don't see me. He's not there. He must have went back inside. I start walking across the lawn to the neighbor's house. The grass is wet. It hasn't rained in days. I look down, and the green grass is red. I squat down and run the palm of my hand over the grass and turn my palm up so I can see: Blood. I look back down at a trail of blood from the one house, back between the two houses. The trail goes back to where Angellous was washing the knives up at the other house. I stand back up and follow the blood trail back into the second house and up the step to the front door: wide open. Foyer, living-room, a hallway straight in front of me, but the blood trail leads up the stairs to the right.

"I gotta see this, so up I go, up the stairs. They wrap back over the front door, then across the living-room, down above the hall. As I come around the balcony, there's a room on the left.

I open slowly, wondering what horrors I will see this time. A teenager's room. A teenage boy's room, but no boy. Some really cool Grateful Dead posters, but no kid. I walk out the room to the hallway, turn left, and walk on down the hall, following the blood trail, which leads to a closed door to my right. I open the door, following the blood and I walk in. I find the teenage boy. Now that is twisted.

"There is a woman hanging from the ceiling. Her arms are pulled back and up behind her back and are tied at the wrist. Her left leg is pulled up behind her and Her ankle is tied to her wrist with what looks to be half inch nylon rope, hung from a big hook in the ceiling. The boy's hands are tied over his head and latched on the same hook as the woman. Another rope is tied around their waist, binding them together, then extending up over her back, under her hung arms, and tied around her throat. Both of them are all cut up. As I walk around to the other side of their bodies. Is he, yeah, he is. The boy's schmeckel is inside her and dripping. He must of just died getting off.

"I walked back out of the bathroom and on down the hall. The last door is a master bedroom. Thankfully no bodies. There are pictures of the woman and the teenage-boy from a baby all the way to present. I guess I was right. That's just sick, Mother and Son. Ewe (that is one hell of a lesson, keep it in the family. A family that sticks together stays together. Incest is the best.) I don't know. Really, it's just, ewe. If he was still alive I would ask him, but the dripping says enough.

"Where's the father / husband? I'm curious just how many bodies are in the kitchen next door. I hear the Shitty Rust Bucket starting up. Angellous must be leaving. I say to myself, 'For- get this dude, I'm outta here.' Mumbling as I'm going down the steps, 'Freaking psycho.' As I get to the front door, I see Angellous going down the road, so I run to my truck and haul ass. The sun is setting. If it's Saturday I should be in Arizona by Monday afternoon.

***

"Back on rt.480 west, at the junction of rt.80 west, I stop for gas. Fill-up and go. Running 80, gotta stop for gas and grub. As I'm filling up I see a sign says Toulon, Illinois eight miles. I realize where I am and that it's now Sunday night. Gas nozzle clicks. I turn to unhook (and surprise) Angellous is standing directly behind me.

"I say, 'Say something next time, so I know you're there. You dam-near gave me a heart attack.'

"Angellous says, 'Okay, something.'

"'Freaking smart ass.'

"'You early! You not suppose to be here, not till tomorrow!'

"'That's not all a bad thing. I get some down time to unwind from driving.'

"'Well, come on. You unwind with a glass of Whiskey on a soft couch.'

"'Alright. Lead the way!'

"We get back in our trucks, pull out on rt.80 west following Angellous. "I can't seem to get away from this Back Woods Fucking Hillbilly." Sign says Toulon two miles. "I wonder what he has to show me, and how in the hell can I get out of this?

"Been driving about an hour, one and a half hours down a long winding desolate dirt road. He's slowing down and turning down another dirt road. I haven't seen a house in miles. Turning again. Draut Road. Wow, this is out in Bumble Fuck J-bib. A few more minutes, 'dam, now that's a house.' The road, Draut Rd., is not a road, it's a driveway. We pull up and park out by the barn. Wait, no it's not a barn. It's a garage. There's a barn behind the house, way off in the back of a field on the right. A ranch house. It's huge, gotta be three thousand square feet easy.

"'Angellous, is this all yours?'

"'Yes, now about that Whiskey.'

"We walk in through the side door. I'm blown away. This is right out of Star's Digest or something. As we walk through the pantry into the enormous kitchen, at the far end past the three tier center-island counter, is an open dividing wall with a Granite counter top leading into the living room. I walk past the column at the beginning of the open wall, two steps down out of the kitchen / hallway into the living room. On the left opposite of the open dividing wall is a full bar. To the right over the fireplace is a seventy inch flat screen TV.

"Angellous says, 'I'll give you the ten cent tour, while the Whiskey is chilling.'

"We walk back up the two steps into the main hallway, just opposite the living room. Across the hall is another hallway. Just to the left is a full bathroom. A couple feet past the bathroom on the left, there's an office / library. Further down the hall, to the right is a big guest room. Immediately in front of me is the last door, a double door that opens into the master bedroom, with its own bathroom which has a stand-up shower / steam shower and a jacuzzi all in stone. We walk back down the main hall toward the kitchen and turn down the other hallway. First door is to the basement. Just past the door is a dining room to the right with a sun-room after it. To the left, on the opposite side of hall is an- other door, closed, and at the end of the hall is the foyer and front door. Angellous opens the closed door: it's a den and we walk in.

"Holy Shit, I'm in Love. On one wall there are dagger's and athame's. On another wall, swords and axes. The third wall was full of shot guns, rifles and pistols. Adjacent to the fourth wall, were two recliners and an end table between them. A coffee table was pulled up and in toward the recliners. The last ten feet or so of that same wall, is a glass cooler. It's filled with cigars, pot and gun powder. So we go back into the living-room. Angellous pours two four-finger glasses of chilled Whiskey. As we sip from our glasses, we watch the Devils win again.

"Angellous says, 'So, like the house?'

"Laughingly I replied, 'Like it. I might kill for something like it.'

"'Wait till you see the rest.'

"'The rest. What is there, servants? Slaves?'

"'Tomorrow, Gavin, tomorrow. Take the guest room down on the right. See you in the morning!'

"'Alright then.' I said, as I strolled on down the hall.

"I go into the guest-room and lay down. Monday morning and I wake up to silence and the smell of coffee. Get up on over to the bathroom and wash up, then I walk out to the kitchen, to get me a cup of that fine-smelling coffee.

"As I enter the kitchen, Angellous says, 'Coffee?' Holding up a cup.

"'Morning. That would be fine, thank you.'

"'Steak and Eggs?'

"'Now that would be great, that is if they are already made

up. Don't go through any trouble for me.'

"'No trouble. Eat up and then I'll show you the rest of the place.'

"We finished with breakfast and a second cup of coffee. Angellous collects the plates, rinses them off in the sink, and then places them in the dishwasher. Angellous and I walk on out through the pantry, out to the driveway, and on up to the three car garage. (or so I thought) I follow Angellous in the garage. It's like a car dealer's mechanic shop: every tool you can think of, from auto to big rigs, from septic and well tools to every last tool for building a house.

"We walk out of the garage, across the field, and out to the barn. There are stables as we walk in with three horses. Just past the horses and one empty stall, there are a couple of pink potbelly pigs on the right side. On the left there are about a half a dozen brown cows. I see a door in the floor, so I ask Angellous, 'What's the door for?'

"Angellous says with a shit-eating grin, 'Later, I got one more thing I just gotta show you.'

"So we leave the garage and walk on out and around back of the garage, through the hedgerow, on this beaten dirt path and walk a few hundred yards where we come to another garage.

"Angellous says, 'Grab that door for me!'

"Then both of us pull open this god-awful huge door.

"Angellous says, 'There she is, my pride: 1961 Barracuda. There's my Briggs Big Rig. Oh ya and there's my new pickup, a Hunter Green 2006 Dodge Ram 1500 Pickup with eight ft. bed, standard factory package.'

I say to Angellous, 'That Pickup looks like mine,' and go on to say, 'You really got a great thing here. Thank you for your hospitality; however, I must be on my way!'

"Angellous answers, 'If you gotta. But you gonna miss the

best part!'

"'Alright. What is it you talking about?'

"'The show. Come on. You'll see!'

"We walk on back to the barn. Angellous opens the door and looks at me with the same shit-eating grin he had before when I asked him about the floor door. He walks over to one of the corrals, picks up two sticks, and wraps a couple of rags around the sticks, and then dips them in an oil drum, then he hands one to me.

"Angellous asked, 'Got a light?'

"here."

"Angellous lights both oil-soaked torches, leans down and opens the door in the floor by lifting it up to the left, and walks on down the steps. The walls and steps are all made of stone, boulders to be precise. We get to the bottom and Angellous lights a torch in the wall, then continues to light two more torches, as we walk down this stone boulder hallway. We come to an opening. Angellous lights a few more as he walks around the room. As the torches are lit, this massive room appears to be made of boulders and cement.

"Angellous says, 'Well?'

"I look around what looks like an Old-Fashion Torture Chamber. There is a wooden table with rope tied to a big wheel on one end and straps of leather on the other end. A two-piece Stock that splits in the middle of four holes that are cut in it, with a half circle iron strap over the top. It looks like it opens swinging up and locks when closed. There are Chains anchored to the wall and other Chains to the floor. There are Ropes and Pulleys hanging from the ceiling. A Steel Cage hung on the wall. A bunch of Whips, Chain and Leather Whips all different sizes. Metal Collars, different Mouth Gags: a metal roll, about the size of a roll of quarters, with straps. A ball with holes in it and straps attached to it. A solid ball with straps. There are some Cattle Prods and Branders, Knives. Something shaped like a Pear. A few other things. I have no idea what they are, but by the looks of things, I could only guess.'

"Again; thank you for your hospitality; however, I must be on my way!'

"Angellous says, 'I understand. Just know this, if you gotta leave, I got me a new pickup.'

"'I guess I'll be staying a bit!'

"'The guest bedroom is yours.'

"'I thank you. I think I'll retire for the evening.'

"I start to walk back out and Angellous douses the torches. We get back up to the barn. Angellous is behind me and closes the door in the floor. We then proceed to walk out of the barn and back to the house. For some reason Angellous did not close this huge barn door. Now back at the house there is food and wine on the kitchen-table. I ask, 'You have a cook?'

"Angellous says, 'Or something.'

"So we feast. I help clear the table. Angellous brings over a bottle of Whiskey and two glasses. After the drink, I excuse my- self and retire for the night.

"Morning. 5:30 comes quick. Tuesday morning I ask myself, 'How am I gonna get out of here?' I wash up and head out of the bathroom and back into the bedroom to get dressed. Now dressed, I go to leave the room and the door is locked. 'What The Fuck!' I start knocking on the door.

"I yell out. 'Angellous. Hello.' The door unlocks. I walk out and say, 'You don't have to lock the door, you know.'

"Angellous answers, 'Breakfast first, then you help. Earn your keep!'

I didn't know what to say. I just sat down and ate. We cleared the table and finished our second cup of coffee.

"Then Angellous said, 'Let's Go!'

3
DISAGREEMENT

"We walked out the house, out to his new pick up that looked identical to mine. It even had the black canopy covering the bed of the truck.

"Angellous said, 'Get in!'

"So I do and I asked, 'Any particular place we going?'

"'Just the barn.'"

***

Back at the Bar, Kasey Jones pub & grub

The Cops interrupt as usual and ask, "Why don't you just leave?"

I answered, "I just watched this Psycho brutally rape and slaughter four Families. Fuck you, just leave.'

"Well how you get away?"

"If you let me, I'll tell y'all."

Now

"I said to Angellous, 'I don't know what sick shit you into, but I assure you, I'm not.'

"Angellous replies, 'That's okay, you'll see! Just you wait. You'll see and you will wanna try it your self!'

“So we finally get to the Barn. Get out the truck. I notice Angellous is unstrapping the canopy and rolling it back toward the cab. He proceeds in opening the tailgate of the pickup. Grabs a rope that was laying against the tailgate.

“Angellous says to me, ‘Well, gonna lend a hand? Pull the fucking rope!’

“So I do, as Angellous and I pull this rope, dragging out this girl. The rope is tied around her waist, down the front of her, through between her knees and down to her bound ankles, as if in a squatting position. I notice her hands are bound behind her back at the wrist. Then the rope continues up her back, wrapped around her neck. Angellous grabs a hold of the rope between her hands and neck. With his other hand, grabs her arm, picks her up over his shoulder and walks to the Barn door.

“Angellous says, ‘Open the door. Light up the torches and give me one!’

“‘Alright, alright, just wait,’ I say as I’m looking for a knife, for she is choking.

“Angellous, with a grin, said, ‘I know, the faster he gets the torch. the sooner you get to breathe.’

“I get the torches and light them, then I think, ‘Maybe I should take my time. Suffocation would be better than.’ Then I gave one of the torches to Angellous. I open the floor door. Down the boulder stairs we go. Down the stone hallway into the room, that dungeon. Angellous drops the girl on the dirt floor and walks around lighting the torches. I notice there are two doors on the right. They are about waist high with little doors about knee high and a foot wide.

“‘Hey Angellous, what are these for?’

“‘Here, I’ll show you.’

“Angellous walks over to me and the doors, squats down, unlocks the door, then stands up and walks backward, opening the door.

"Angellous says, 'After you, come on.'

"So I reached in with the torch and I hesitate, then Angellous shoved me in, closed and locked the door. It's a little holding room.

"Angellous said, 'Question me.'

"'Hey, open the fucking door!'

"'you wanted to know what's in there. Now you know. You and a bucket.'

"'Let me the fuck out.'

"Angellous hands me a video recorder and says, 'Behave and record what I tell you to or I will take your Bucket!'

"Angellous takes a hold of the rope up by her neck and drags her over to this machine, this device. He cuts the rope between her ankles and wrist, cuts the rope going from her wrist up to her neck, leaving the rope separately tied around her neck, ankles and her wrist, then takes this chain with a hook and slides the hook between her hands through latching on the bind of her wrist, then walks over to the pillar and pulls the other end of the chain, raising her arms up behind her back up towards the ceiling. As she screams, the chain goes 'Click, Click, Click, Click' and stops with her shoulders almost dislocated, leaving her feet barely on the ground.

"Angellous walks over to a table. He's rummaging through tools, knives and devices. He stops; he's not moving. He turns, holding a long fillet knife.

"I yell. 'No, Angellous, No. It's okay, girl, just look over here, Look at me.'

"He turns with this sadistic expression and a cold dead stare, walks back over to the girl. She's screaming and bouncing around. Tears are running down her face, and fall unto the floor like rain.

"I ask the girl, 'What's your name?'

"The girl, hysterically, she replies, 'My Name is Callisto. Please, let me go. I don't understand, what did I do? Please, I obeyed! I did everything you asked! Please, I only went for a walk! I swear, it was only a walk! PLEASE.'

"Callisto has calf-high Black boots with buckle strap, really tight black jeans, covering really great legs with a tight, perky, perfect undercut Ass. I don't think you could even get a finger between her skin and those jeans. Wearing a sagged studded belt around her waist 80's style. A really tight belly shirt and a belly ring with a chain traveling down in her pants. Her Breast gotta be full C's. They look perky and firm. Best tits I've ever seen! A black metal collar around the base of her neck, under the tied rope. Bracelets (a lot of bracelets) with a running chain to her middle finger, black painted long fingernails. Long curly, silky black hair with a purple streak and really bright green eyes, bright as if they glowed.

"Angellous looks at me and tells me, 'She's mine!'

"As Angellous slides his left hand in the neck collar and down over her right shoulder, out the bottom of the sleeve, he takes the fillet knife with his right hand, and slides the knife along the side of his left fingers, until the blade came out the bottom of the sleeve. She's jumping around and screams 'Ow.' He must of nicked her. Blood is dripping down her arm. Slowly Angellous pulls the knife up and down, cutting the shoulder-strap of the shirt. Front right shoulder of the shirt falls forward, about half- way down the strap lines, showing the top of her right breast. Drags the back edge of the knife down her arm and then licks the dripping blood off her shoulder.

"Angellous wiped the tears from her face and wiped her nose with his left hand. He takes a hold of her chin, staring into her face. Callisto begs him, 'Please, please,' while crying. Angellous leans in and kisses her, a soft and gentle kiss almost that of seduction.

"Angellous takes a step back and forces a ball in her mouth, pulls the straps of the ball gag around her head, latching them tight. He releases the chain, lowering her arms to the center of her back. Angellous, with his right hand, grabs a hold of the rope that is tied around her ankles, whisks up her feet, hooking her tied ankles on the same hook her tied hands are bound to. As she screams in pain, her shoulders bulge, as if one good jerk would dislocate them.

"She's hanging by her ankles and wrists about three feet off the ground (I can still hear her crying and mumbling). Angellous slowly pulls the chain, raising her higher. Click. Click. Click. Click. Click. Finally he stops. She's now about five feet off the ground. Angellous put out three of the five torches, then takes one torch as he walks out.

"I yell at him. 'Hey, let me out of here, come on, open the Door. It's not funny anymore!'

"Angellous ignores me. The light grows dimmer as he walks down the hall. We can barely see each other.

"I tell her, 'I'll get us outta here, Just hold on.'

"Callisto replies, 'M m ah m ma mm.' She's mumbling, crying, and coughing, still with a ball gag in her mouth.

"Time goes by. I don't know how long, must have been a day or two. Angellous is coming. Callisto starts panicking as the hallway gets brighter, now hysterical as Angellous walks in the room, lighting the other torches. He comes over, squats down, unlocks and opens the little door, sliding in a plate of food, and then closes and locks the little food door.

"Angellous stood up and said, 'Let me know when you are done, we will start.'

"Starving, I grabbed the food and ate. I look out, and Angellous removed the ball gag out of Callisto's mouth, and he is trying to hand-feed her. She is trying to bite his hand. Angellous smacks her face lightly with his left hand, and softly says, 'Stop, eat!' Again, with his right hand, he attempts to feed her. She eats a little. Angellous caresses her cheek and runs his fingertips down her neck onto her collarbone. With her mouth full of food, Callisto spits it back in his face. Angellous grunts, steps back, and walks over to the table and drops the plate.

"'I have finished eating, thank you. Now how about letting me out?'

"'Camera on? If not, let's get it going.'

"Angellous walks over to the chain and lowers her down one foot then walks back to her, lifts her chin to see her face, and wipes her tears. As she tries to bite his hand, he slaps her again, stares in her face for a moment, then walks to her side.

"Callisto is bouncing and jumping around screaming 'Get off of me.'

"Angellous unhooks her ankles, lowering her feet to the floor. He squats down and tries to untie her ankles as she tries to kick him but can barely lift up her leg. Angellous turns his back in against the front of her body. Angellous reaches down with his right hand. She's squirming.

"Callisto yells, 'Don't touch me, you freak.'

"Angellous grabs her right leg, lifting it forward, leaving the left foot barely touching the ground. She moans. Angellous starts unbuckling her right calf-high Boot. Callisto's cursing him out and is flailing around. He pulls off her boot, sets her right leg down, then picks up her left leg. She screams in pain as he slides off her left boot. Now bootless, her stocking-covered toes just touching the ground, and her arms holding her weight. Callisto's arms appear as if they could not possibly hold any more weight, as her shoulders look like they are already dislocated.

"With tears in her eyes and full of pain, she is hysterically trying to get loose while cursing at Angellous. He's just standing there with this blank expression on his face, this look in his eyes that of a kid in a candy store. He turns to the table, turns on a radio. He puts in a cassette tape. It sounds like, 'It's Johnny Rebel' singing, 'Get the rope.'

"'You got any Rodney Carrington?'

"'Mixed tape. Got it all!'

"And on comes, David Allan Coe. Which you could barely hear over her fussing and begging.

"Angellous says, 'Stop the video!'

"He sat down in front of the stone column. Couple hours go by, just staring at her without saying a word the whole time. He gets up and walks back over to Callisto, lifts her head, staring in her face for a moment.

"Angellous asked, 'What is it you want?' "Callisto answered, 'Let me go? Please?' "'What is it you need?'

"'Pee, I have to Pee!'

"Angellous steps back and to the right side of her, with his left hand holding the hook, with his right hand lifting her rope-bound wrist off the hook. She screams, tries to pull away and falls. Angellous stands her back up and wipes off her pants. With his left hand on the top of her left shoulder, with his right hand holding her bound wrist, he walks her over to the corner.

"Angellous said, 'The bucket is yours!' He walks around to the front of her and says, 'Behave or I will take away your bucket!'

"Angellous reaches down and starts unbuttoning her skin-tight pants. He kneels down and starts slowly pulling and shifting her pants down. As her pants come over the bridge of her ass, Callisto tries to kick him.

"Angellous catches her shin and says, 'That's one, Next your bucket!'

“Angellous continues to pull down her pants, slowly down past her ass to the beginning of her thighs and stops. He pauses and breathes in heavily while licking his lips, then pulls her pants down to her knees. He reaches up, sliding his hand up the outside of her thighs to her waist and slowly pulls down her black lace panties, down to meet her scrunched up pants around her knees. He reaches behind her, grabbing the bucket, and drags it up be- hind her legs. Angellous stands up and smiles, then walks behind her, sliding his hands and arms between her arms and her ribs out in front of her, crossing his arms, taking a hold of each of her breasts, a breast in each hand, with his chest up against her back.

“Angellous says, ‘Sit back. I have you!’

“As Callisto nervously tries to pee, Angellous enjoys his grip. She finishes, and Angellous stands her back up, opens his hands, releasing her breasts, and pulls his right arm out. He takes a step to her left, pulls a tissue out of his back pocket. While staring in her face, he reaches up between her legs with the tissue and wipes her. He throws the tissue in the bucket, pulls his left arm out and squats down on her side, turns her body to face him, and pulls up her black lace panties.

“Stands up and walks her over to an old, wooden chair with leather straps. (kind of reminds you of an old Porch chair.) He sits her down, strapping her in around her stomach, then squats down, strapping in both her shins against the legs of the chair, gets up and walks out of the room and down the stone hallway.

“After what seemed like a couple of hours gone-by, Angellous walks back in with two brown paper bags. He comes over to me, squats in front of my holding room door, unlocks and opens the little door, and slides in a plate of grub. (it’s Lo-mien and a bottle of water.) closes and locks the little food door.

“He then stands up and walks over to Callisto. He pulls out

the same plate of Chinese food and a bottle of water. Angellous pulls out a little fork and begins feeding her. Callisto is now so hungry she's choking as she barely chews the food as he feeds her. Angellous pulled back the plate, placing the fork on the plate. Feeds her some of the bottled water. He continues to slowly feed her until she finishes the Lo-mien and then gives her a little more water to drink. He then gets up and starts putting out the torches, leaving one lit in the room. As he walks out, we watch a light get dimmer and dimmer. We can barely see each other. Callisto's just crying. I'm trying to calm her saying anything I can think of. I even tried to tell her everything will be all right."

4
CONSEQUENCE

"No matter what I say, it seems to make no difference. It's as if Callisto doesn't even hear me. Time goes by. Callisto falls asleep. It's hard to know how long he's been gone. We are both starving of thirst and hunger. I really felt bad for Callisto. I at least have use of my bucket, as where she is still strapped to that chair, after drinking a bottle of water and eating all that Lo-mien. "Hallway's getting brighter, or is it just my eyes? No it's Angellous. He lights the torches around the room and walks over to me. He reaches through the window of the door with his fingers and hands me another memory card. It's marked Saturday. With his palm up, snapping his fingers, he says, 'Give me Tuesday's memory card.' So not to end up like Callisto, for me to keep my bucket, I hand him the memory card. Then he walks out of the room, back down the hallway. About a half hour goes by, and I hear screaming.

"'Let go of me! Fuck you, you fucking ugly mother fucker! I'll fucking kill you! Get off me!' "Callisto wakes up, panicking. Angellous is dragging this girl into the room by her bound hands, as she kicks and frolics around. Angellous drags the new girl to the chain with the hook that Callisto was at first hanging on. He lifts her up, slides the hook between her hands, latching the hook on the rope binding her wrist, then walks quickly over to the chain coming down the column, and pulls the chain with all the strength in his arm. Click Click Click Click Click Click Click Click Click Click Click Click, until she is standing with her arms extended straight up over her head. Then he pulls again, slowly, Click. Click. Click. Click, lifting her clear off the ground. She's bouncing and kicking trying to kick Angellous as he stares and pokes her legs, laughing.

"The girl's screaming, 'You fucking cock-sucker! I get out of here, I'm gonna kill you! I'll kill you!'

"Angellous looks at me and says, 'Feisty. That's good for your first one, Gavin!'

"Angellous turns and walks over to the table, mumbling. There is something in his hand. He turns around and walks back to the new girl. It's another mouth-gag. She tries to kick him. Angellous swats her leg, spinning her around. He grabs a hold of her arm to stop her from spinning. Her back to his front, now to her side, he takes the mouth-gag in his right hand reaches to the top of her head and flips the strap to the back of her head. He then holds the strap with his left hand behind her head and pulls the mouth-gag down over her face with his right hand, forcing it into her mouth. She tries to fight it, wiggling her head around, but it is no use. The cylinder gag is wedged in her mouth as he tightens the strap buckle behind her head.

"Angellous turned away and walked over to the half-door next to me. He squats, unlocks the door, and reaches inside. Something is sliding. He's pulling out a drum. He drags the drum a few more feet, then opens it, pulling the lid off. He walks off to the left towards the corner of the room and walks back with a bucket, dips the bucket in the drum, lifts the bucket up and out of the drum. Then he walks over to Callisto, holding the rim of the bucket with his left hand and the bottom of the Bucket with his right, with the sweep from his back, right side to his front, tossing the liquid contents at her, splashing her mid-drift between her breasts, and above her waist. It's water. Callisto loses her breath, gasps as the water hits, splashing up in her face and soaking her from her perfect C-size breasts down into her lap. That water must really be cold!

"Angellous says, 'Gavin, I let you out, you going to behave?' "'Yes, yes. I'll behave!'

"Angellous sets down the bucket, walks across past my door. I hear chains rattling, getting closer and closer. He drops the chains on the floor, picks back up the bucket, and refills it in the drum, then walks over to the new girl. He douses her with the cold water, as she flails about he sets down the bucket and walks back over to my door, squats down, and unlocks it. He stands up, as he opens the door, and he kicks the chain into the room.

"Angellous says, 'Open the leg iron and strap it on!'

"'So I do. Then I walked, hunched over, to get through the door. I went over to Callisto.'

"I asked, 'Are you okay?'

"Callisto replied, 'Get me out of here!'

"'I'm trying!'

"Angellous says, 'She's mine. Yours is hanging!'

"I turned to Angellous as he walked over to me. He grabs my arm and walks me to the new girl, then hands me the fillet knife. "Angellous says, 'Cut Her! Slow and shallow! Place the blade on the top of the arm up by her shoulder! Gently, pull back and down! A short and clean cut. Then you can have a taste!' "'No, I won't man, NO!'

"'You will! Or you will be hanging there! And she will cut you!' With an empty dead stare, Angellous continues to say, 'Your decision?'

"So I look at the new girls face. She's crying and trying to beg me not to cut her, but with that gag wedged in her mouth, I can't understand a word. I pull out the mouth-gag cylinder and slide it down past her chin.

"Angellous says, 'That's my boy. Now slow and clean. Don't hesitate, a smooth cut!'

"I walk around to the side of her, almost behind her. I reach up with the Fillet knife, laying the blade on her bicep below her shoulder, trying not to apply pressure. I begin dragging the blade down and across cutting into her skin, trying to stay shallow, as the blood runs down the side of her body and on down the side of her stomach. The new girl screams, 'Ow' and cries.

"Angellous says, 'A taste!'

"I look at him and grab a hold of the new girl. I lean in. I place my tongue against her skin and lick the blood off of her skin, from the bottom of her ribs up to the cut on her shoulder.

"She is really crying now, begging, crying, and begging, 'Let me go. Please, just let me go?'

"Angellous says, 'Smack her face! Tell her to stop crying or I will take my time. Tell her!'

"So I tell her. 'If you don't stop, I will have to take my time!' The new girl calms down. I ask her, 'What is your name?'

"The new girl says, 'Marriessa! My name is Marriessa. Let me go, please?'

"Callisto says, 'Stop. You have to calm down or it will get worse!'

"Angellous takes a knife, then says, 'Take her shoes off and place them in a bag over there.'

"I noticed Angellous is pointing to the shelf on the wall. I slowly take off her shoes, Right shoe first, then the left. (They are black-strapped two and a half inch stilettos.) I walk over to the shelf and place the shoes in the bag.

"Angellous says, 'Over here. Bring the bag over here!'

"Angellous opens an old chest box. As I dropped the bag of shoes, he grabbed me by the arm and walked me back to Marriessa.

"Angellous says, 'Now the jewelry. Take it off and put the jewelry in the box on the floor against the column!'

"Marriessa is getting hysterical and screaming, 'Get off me! Why you listening to him? Stop!'

"I get the bucket, flip it over, and stand on it. I take off her cross necklace and tennis bracelet and pull out as I step down and take her scrunchy. Step back up on the bucket, taking her rings off one by one, then step down, turn, and walk over to the third column and bend down over the box, dropped the jewelry in. I stood back up and walked back to Angellous.

"I ask, 'And now?'

"Angellous says, 'Back in your room. Wait!'

"As he hands me the fillet knife, Angellous says, 'Take a knife and cut her shirt off, or it's back in the hold with ya.'

"I take the knife, walk to the front of Marriessa. I tell her, 'I'm sorry.'

"I reach up and cut the left shoulder-strap of her string halter top.

"Marriessa is pleading, 'Please, please stop? Don't do this, please?'

"I reach over to the right shoulder and cut the last strap of the halter top, still wet and clinging to her breasts. I pulled her halter top, from the bottom up, scrunching it up around the bottom of her breasts, exposing all of her stomach. I slide the knife between her smooth olive skin and the bunched up shirt in my hand, and pull her shirt tight to cut it free. I let go of her shirt. I watch as it falls back onto her. Her rack is still holding up her top. I take a hold of what's left of her halter top. Gently, I pull the top off, exposing her bra-covered breasts.

"I asked him, 'Where does this go?'

"Angellous says, 'Her bra too, then in a bag and into the chest box with the shoes.'

"Marriessa yells, 'Stop, you piece of shit. Stay away from me!'

“I turned back to Marriessa. She’s trying to kick me. I reached down, grabbed her legs, forcing them together squirreling them up in my right arm as she is flailing around. I slowly place the knife on her skin, over the top of her right breast, sliding under the bra-strap, so she feels the cold of the blade. I pull up and out, cutting the right bra-strap away from her body.

“Now, sliding the knife on her skin across her chest over the top of her right breast and down between, then from the inside up over the top of her left breast under her bra strap, I cut the strap away from her body. I leaned back, still holding her legs, and handed Angellous back the knife. I slid my left hand on up the side of her stomach, slide my hand underneath her bra cupping her right breast, still holding her legs with my right arm, as she is bouncing and flailing around, I let go of her right tit and slide my hand to the center of her boozums, and unlatch the bra clip, her bra separates and comes off her breasts. Her bra falls to the dirt floor. Her breasts are beautiful. I guess a size B. Not as nice as Callisto’s melon-shaped breasts. Marriessa’s breasts are pear- shaped. I let down her legs, and I pick up her halter top and bra off the floor.

“I walk over to place them in a bag, a few more steps, and drop the bag in the old chest box. I walk back over to Marriessa and I put this Cylinder-gag back in her mouth. As I watch Marriessa, she begins crying. Her tears run down her face, dripping off her chin onto her breasts, rolling down to the bottom of her breast and dripping off onto the floor.

“Angellous says, ‘Over here!’

“I walked to the far stone wall where Angellous is standing. I ask, ‘Yes. What now?’

“Angellous says, ‘You see that shackle? Put it on or go back in the holding room!’

“So I put on the shackle and locked it. ‘I’m not going back in that holding room!’ Angellous goes over to the holding room, gets out my bucket and the video camera, brings them over to me, then walks over to Callisto. He places his left hand on her right knee and unstraps her ankle from the leg of a chair. With his left hand, he lifts up her leg, and with his right hand he pulls her pants off. As he's lifting her leg, pulling her foot up 'n' in, out of her pants, Callisto tries to kick Angellous, but does not succeed. "Angellous says, 'Don't try it again, or you'll be punished!' "Angellous then re-straps her ankle of her left leg down against the chair. He stands up and walks to the other side of Callisto, kneels back down, unstrapping her right leg, and with his left hand he lifts her leg up, takes a hold of the cuff of her pants, and slowly pulls her pants down her right leg and off her foot. With her pants off, her right leg re-strapped to the chair, Angellous kneels in the front of her, lifts her left leg, and places her foot on his top right thigh. He's sliding his hand from the inside of her right ankle, continuing up the inside of her calf up to her knee. Then he continues to slide his hand halfway up the inside of Callisto's thigh. She tries to move and goes nowhere. As Angellous lifts her left leg with his right hand and tries to slide his left hand further up the inside of her thigh, Callisto lifts her left leg and kicks Angellous in his chest, knocking him backwards on his ass.

"Callisto says, 'Don't touch me!'

"As Angellous picked himself up off the floor and stands up, Callisto said, 'You're not even a man. You're Pathetic! You hear me? You fucking asshole. You're pathetic!'

"Angellous smiles and grabs her right leg. Callisto's still trying to kick Angellous as he pulls up and pushes out her leg, opening her thighs. He steps in towards her and turns his back against the front of her torso. He wraps his right arm around her calf, almost enabling her leg. As he looks over his shoulder, Callisto is really trying to pull away. Angellous, with his left hand, grabs a hold of her big toe and pulls it towards her left leg, dislocating her big toe.

“Callisto screams in pain and begs, ‘Please stop? I’ll listen. Please, stop!’

“Angellous says, ‘Understand, or do I break another toe?’

“‘I understand. Yes, yes. I won’t kick you again! Just stop, please stop?’

“‘Very well.’

“Angellous reset her big toe and dropped her leg. He stood back up and turned around to face Callisto. He then squats down and slides his hand on the inside of her right knee. He continues sliding his hand up the inside of her thigh, gently sliding about three-quarters the way up. Callisto was just crying. Angellous stops his hand. While staring aimlessly at her thigh, he traces the infinity sign with his fingertips. He continues to graze her skin with his fingertips down to her knee, leans back, and continues down her shin all the way down to her ankle. He then straps her right leg back against the chair. Angellous stands up, walks be- hind Callisto who is frantically crying. He places both his hands on her shoulders, massaging her neck and tense shoulders. A minute goes by and he stops. He looks over at me and then be- gins laughing as he starts walking over to Marriessa.

“Angellous says, ‘Consequences!’

“Angellous takes a hold of Marriessa’s ankles. He begins to slide his hands up between her ankle-length skirt, from the outside of her calf’s. He continues sliding his hands up the outside of her legs up past her knees, all the way up her thighs to her waist. Then he lets go and pulls his hands back, watching her ankle-long skirt fall back to where it once lay.

“He raises his hands back up to her smooth and toned stomach. He steps in and continues raising his hands up against the smooth skin of her body. He comes to stop, as his hands cup both of her breasts. Marriessa is flailing around. She is trying to knee him with her left leg, but he is too close for it to have any effect. Angellous grabs her left leg with his right hand, pulls out a knife from his back pocket, and with his left hand, he drags the back- edge of the knife down from the top inside of her thigh. While she is trying to pull away, he stops about four inches above her knee and slides the blade about two inches into the side of her thigh. Marriessa tries to scream.

"Angellous asked, 'Enough?'

"Marriessa nods and mumbles, 'Yes.'

"Angellous pulls out the knife, looks at her leg bleeding. He pulled her leg up and put his mouth over the cut. I can see him swallowing three, four, five swallows, drinking the blood off of her leg. She is still bleeding. The blood is slowly running down her leg, down to her ankles, and dripping onto the dirt floor. Angellous lets her leg back down, then he walks over to the table and he turns with a really big needle and string in his hands, and walks back to Marriessa.

"Marriessa's hysterically mumbling, 'No. Please. No?'

"Angellous reaches down and grabs a hold of her left leg, raising up her foot until it sets against his hip. He once again licked the blood off her leg, from the bottom of her thigh up to the top of the cut. He threads string into the eye of the needle. He then starts by sticking the point of the needle into her skin, from below the bottom of the open wound through the opening into the other side of the open wound and up, out of her skin, pulling the threaded needle until it's out, then back over to the bottom and sticks the needle in again, from the bottom of the wound up through the opening into the other side and out, pulling it out yet again. He tugs on the thread until the wound is closed, looping the needle through its own thread and pulling taut, tying off the two stitches. Marriessa is calming down. Angellous takes his knife and cuts the string free from her leg. He lifts her foot up off of his hip and lets her leg back down, then walks out of the room. "An hour or so goes by, and he comes back into the room with the plastic bag of what looked like a bag of ice, continues to walk over to Callisto and wraps the ice bag from the bottom of her foot, up around her big toe, and over onto the top of her foot. Then with a torch in his left hand, he walks around the room put- ting out the other torches with a cup on a rod that he's holding in his right hand, leaving one torch lit in the far corner as he walks out. The room grows dimmer as he walks on down the stone hallway. We hear the slamming of the floor door.

"Callisto says to me, 'Why are you listening to him? How can you do that to her? Why didn't you try and kill him?'

"'I've been down here about a week or more. If I do what he tells me. He said, 'I get to live.' Try to get some sleep. You will need to keep up your strength!'

5
OBEDIENCE

"It's been about a day or two now. We hear the floor door opening. Angellous walks in the room with two bags, sets them down on the tool table, and picks up a bucket. Walks over to the drum, dips the bucket into the drum, filling it up with water, lifts it up and out of the drum. With the full bucket of water, he walks over to Callisto, looks at her and tosses the water, soaking her from the bottom of her head, beginning of her neck, down to her mid-drift, soaking her hips and thighs. He sets the bucket down by the front, bottom leg of the table.

"Then he walks back over to the tool table and opens both bags. As he unloads the bags, I notice it is Chinese food again and six bottles of water. He sets a box and a bottle in Callisto's lap, then brings the other box and a bottle of water over handing them to me. He reaches into his pocket and pulls out a memory card and hands it to me. It's marked Friday. Then he walked back over to Callisto.

"Angellous kneels down on his right knee and picks the box up out of her lap. With his right hand he grabs a bottle and wedges it between her thighs. He pulls out a fork, opens the box and digs into the box, lifts it up under her chin, and feeds her. I believe it's fried rice. We are both so hungry, Callisto and I are barely able to keep our composure. As we find each-other choking while we're trying to swallow, she slows down and continues to eat, savoring every last tasteful bite.

"After a few more bites, Angellous places the box between her knees and pulls the water bottle out from between her thighs, opens and removes the cap. He holds the bottle of water while she drinks. He pulls the bottle slowly away from her lips, careful not to spill any of the water. Then he places the bottle back be- tween her thighs. He takes a napkin out of his right back pocket and wipes her lips and chin. He picks back up the box of fried rice, lifts it up to her chin, and feeds her what was left. He wipes her chin off again, picks up the bottle of water, and raises it to her lips, allowing her to drink the last of the bottled water.

"Angellous stands back up and throws the empty box and empty bottle into the plastic bag by the table. He then walks over to me and, to my surprise, he hands me a key. As he walks back to the table, I unlock the waist shackle, releasing me from the wall. No matter how hard I try to unlock the ankle restraint, the key does not fit, leaving me still chained to the wall by the ankle restraint.

"I walk over to Angellous, dragging a thick, heavy, thirty foot long ankle chain. Angellous hands me a box, bottle, and a fork. Then he walks over to the column. He starts lowering down Marriessa until her feet are on the ground and her knees bent.

"Angellous says to me, 'Feed your girl, but control her!'

"Angellous just walks back and forth, watching, while holding the camera and recording. I walk over to Marriessa. With my right hand, I place the box of rice between her bent knees. With my left hand, I slide my fingers down the soft skin of her stomach, feeling each ripple of her toned abs. I continue sliding my fingers down, down the center, until I come to the waist of her ankle-long skirt. As I slide my fingers between the waist of her skirt and her pooch, gently I pull the waist away from her soft smooth skin and then I wedge the water bottle in place of my fingers.

"Marriessa keeps wiggling around as I slide both my hands gently up the sides of her stomach, over her ribs, up the sides of her breasts, up over the top of her breasts, up her chest plate to her neck. (It's been so long and she's just so,.. mm.) Then I reach up with my right hand, taking a hold of the cylinder mouth gag. With the left hand reaching behind her head, I unbuckle the strap from around her head. I removed her cylinder mouth gag and strap it around her right arm.

"Marriessa says, 'Don't touch me, creep!'

"I reached down with my left hand, grabbing the box of Chinese food out from between her knees. With my right hand, I pull out the bottle of water from her skirt waist, then I walk away.

"Marriessa eagerly yells, 'Wait wait. I'm sorry. Wait.'

"I stopped, turned around, and walked back to her. I put the bottle back between her stomach and her skirt waist. Opened the box of Chinese, pulled out the plastic fork from my back pocket, and I started feeding her. She's wolfing it down. Like Callisto and I did. I tell her, 'Easy.' After she has a few bites, I stop and I place the box between her knees. I pull out the water bottle, unscrew the cap, and hold it for her while she drinks. I put the cap back on the bottle and place it back between her skirt waist and pooch. I continued feeding her the last of the fried rice. Then with my hand I wipe her mouth and chin off.

"I begin sliding my left hand down her neck, down her chest plate, down over her right breast to the bottom, and up under, cupping her breast. (her nipples are really hard.) Marriessa says nothing, just sheds a few tears, so I let go of her breast, reached down and grabbed the bottle of water, unscrewed the cap, and held it while she drank the last of it. When she finished, I walked back to the table and placed the empty box and bottle into the plastic bag, as to throw it out.

"Angellous says, 'Her skirt!'

"I look at Angellous, then turn and walk back to Marriessa.

"Marriessa is begging, 'Please don't? PLEASE? No, NO. Please, No?'

"I walked to the front of Marriessa, and reached around on both sides. With my right hand I take a hold of the waist of her skirt. With my left hand I unzip the five inch zipper of her skirt. With my hands placed on the small of her back, I slide my thumbs down between her skirt and skin, the rest of my fingers over the outside of her skirt, onto the top of her ass and slide to her sides. "Then I begin shifting her skirt down, sliding my hands from the side back to the top of her ass, to the sides, to her ass, until her skirt fell down to her ankles. I squatted down, holding her skirt, and then told her to step out, noticing she is wearing a thong, a red laced thong. Slowly, she tries to step out, so I take a hold of her left calf and lift her foot up and out of her skirt, then set her foot back on the dirt floor. I reached over and took a hold of her right calf, lifting her foot off the floor, pulling the skirt away as the skirt fell off the back of her ankle onto the dirt floor. I lowered her right foot down on the dirt floor. I stood up and walked over, placing her skirt in a bag, then walked over to the old chess box.

"As I opened it, Angellous says, 'You forgot something!'

"I replied, 'Really?'

"'Thong!'

"I walked back over to Marriessa, still with the bag in my right hand. I dropped the bag on the floor and squatted down in front of her.

I look up to Marriessa and say, "I'm sorry."

"Marriessa is crying and has crossed her legs. I place my

hands on the sides of her hips. I began sliding my hands to her front while sliding my fingers between her lace thong and her skin. Then, sliding my fingers back to the crack of her ass, from the crack of her ass back to the front, back to the crack of her ass, as I'm pulling down her red thong, I continue sliding my fingers back and forth from the front to the back, lowering her thong a little more each time, until the waist of the thong was down around the base of her ass. I continued to pull the waist band of her thong down, down around her thighs. I pull a little more, but her panties won't come down with her legs still crossed. I look up.

"Marriessa is crying and begging, mumbling, 'No, no, please stop?'

"I look at Angellous with his left-hand pointer out. He's ro- tating it counterclockwise as if to signal me, 'Come on. Come on.' I look back at Marriessa.

"I tell her, 'Uncross your legs!' Softly I say, 'If you don't, he will uncross your legs for you! I will be the only one touching you!'

"Still crying, Marriessa uncrosses her legs. Slowly I pull her red lace thong down past her knees. (I can smell her. Even with the urine stench you can still smell her fresh cum, she smells pretty great!) She has a thin travel line. I would've thought a diamond or a heart design, but a travel line works. You can tell she is well maintained. I reach up to her waist with my right hand, my left hand on her left leg, and I turn her about halfway around. Man, she has a nice ass: an apple bottom. I continue pulling down her panties from her knees down to her ankles. I lift her legs from under the shins and pull her panties over her ankles and down off her feet, then I set her feet back down on the dirt-floor. I turn and grab the bag the skirt was in and place the red laced panties in the bag as well. I get up and walk over by Angellous and drop the bag in the old chess box.

Angellous is pointing to an old, mechanic's battery charger.

"Angellous says, 'Wheel it over to her. Set it to level III! The sponges are on the table! Fill the bucket!' Pauses for a moment and says, 'I can show you?'

"Thinking he means to do it to me, I pulled the battery charger over to the front of Marriessa, then walked over to the table, grabbed two sponges, and walked back to the charger. Then I picked up an empty bucket and walked to the other side of the room, dipped the bucket into the barrel, filling the bucket with water, lifting it up and out. I carry the full bucket of water back over by Marriessa.

"Angellous says, 'Connect the cables to the sponges, dip them in the bucket of water. By the chain, raise her!'

"Marriessa is now hysterical and frantically trying to unhook the chain hook from her rope-bound wrist. Angellous walked back over to the column, takes a hold of the chain, and pulls: click click click click click click. Raising Marriessa until her toes are barely scraping the dirt floor. I hold a negative clamp of the battery charger cables, squeeze the clamp to open the teeth, then stick the side of the sponge into the open teeth of the clamp, then open my hand, releasing the clamp teeth down into the sponge. I lay the negative cable on the dirt floor. I pick up the positive cable, squeeze in the clamp, opening the teeth of the clamp, sliding the side of the sponge in the opening, and open my hand, releasing the clamp for the teeth to close on the sponge. I turned to the battery charger, I noticed, above the level dial that is set on III, the meter states eight-hundred amps. I pick up the negative cable of the battery charger off the dirt floor. I dipped the negative ca- ble into the water bucket, soaking the sponge, and then I pulled it out. I then dipped the positive cable, soaking this sponge as well. I turned it on.

"I pressed the sponge of the negative cable against the outside of her right leg. Nothing happened. Marriessa is pleading and begging with me not to touch her with the other sponge. I look at Angellous, He just smirked. I turned and looked at Callisto. She was crying quietly to herself. I could still see the tears rolling down her cheeks. Then turned back and look at Marriessa.

"Angellous said, 'Here, I'll show you!'

"So I carefully handed him the Battery charger cable clamps holding the cold, wet sponges. Angellous walks in front of me, looking at Marriessa, her eyes closed and cringing. Angellous quickly turns around and presses both the sponges against my chest. I come to, laying on the dirt floor, Angellous still holding the battery charger cables with the wet sponges, laughing his ass off. I sit up. Damn my chest hurts.

"I say, 'I got it, you fuck!'

"'You sure. I can show you again?'

"'No, no, I got it!'

"So I get up, walk back to Angellous, and take the cables from him. I dipped the negative cable sponge into the bucket of the water first, pulled the sponge out soaking wet, then I dipped the positive cable, soaking that sponge as well. Once again, I press the negative cable, holding the soaked sponge against her right-outer thigh, the water from the sponge dripping down her leg. With the positive cable, I quickly press the wet soaked sponge against the outside of her left thigh and pull it away. Marriessa is flailing around, screaming. I waited a minute or two, then I pressed the negative cable holding the wet sponge against her inside-right thigh.

"Marriessa begs me while crying, 'No please no more!'

"I quickly press the positive cable, holding the other wet sponge against the out-side of her left hip and butt cheek. Marriessa is twitching and violently shaking. This time she cums, pulsating out and down her leg, dripping onto the dirt floor.

“Angellous says, ‘Enough! Turn it off and put it back against the tool table.’

“I happily turn it off. As I wrap up the battery charger, Angellous walks over to Callisto.

“Callisto says to Angellous, ‘I have to go to the bathroom!’

“Angellous squats down, unstrapped her legs, then he unstrapped her waist. He turns to me and says, ‘See this stationary iron restraint. Set it on the rack table!’

“Angellous stands Callisto up. He walks her over by the wall to the bucket. He steps behind her, with his hands on her hips. As he leans down, he slides her black-laced panties down to her knees. He stands back up and slides his arms between her arms and her ribs. He begins to tell her to sit back. As Callisto sits back, Angellous supports her from under her arms, while holding her breast, as she urinates and defecates into her bucket. When she finished, Angellous wrapped his left arm around her, from under her breast, supporting her with his shoulder and head against her back. He reached down and wiped her clean with tissues, then he stood her up and walked her along the wall. He then placed a waist shackle that is anchored to the wall around her hips and padlocked it shut.

“Angellous walked over to me and Marriessa, then over to the column. He began lowering the chain Marriessa is hung from. With her feet firmly on the floor, Angellous walks behind her. He reaches up and lifts her by her bleeding bound wrist, while pulling out the chain hook that she hanged from. Then he turns and effortlessly shoves her into me. Angellous just points to the rack table. I turn her, and we take a few steps. I then grabbed her by the waist and I lifted her up on the table. She starts fussing, wiggling around, trying to get off the table, trying to push me away. Not knowing what he would do to me next, I slapped her in the face and told her to stop.

“Angellous said, ‘Around the neck, wrist, and ankles!’

“I look over at Callisto. She’s walking back and forth against a stone boulder wall trying to undo the waist shackle. I pick up the stationary iron restraint and unlocked it by pulling the pin, separating each side, allowing it to open outward.

“I lifted it up over her head and down around her neck, and began closing it back together. As Marriessa is sitting up on the rack table, I take a hold of her bound wrists, raise them into the wrist opening, and continue to force the stationary restraint closed. I then forced her right leg to bend at the knee and shoved her ankle up. She rolls down onto her right side, as I clamp her ankle into the stationary device. Then I grab a hold of her left leg, pushing her knee away from me as I pull her ankle toward me, forcing her ankle up in the stationary device. Now, with her knees bent up on the outside of her elbows, I finished closing the restraint. I locked it in place by reinserting the pin.

“Angellous says, ‘Roll her on her back. Eat!’

“I said, ‘Eat?’

“Angellous replied, ‘She’s your girl. Go down on her!’

“So I rolled her on her back. Wow, her Cooch is perfect! Plump, juicy lips, almost as if she never had cock before. I can still smell her from when she got off while she was being electrocuted. Marriessa is crying as I start to rub her plump lips with the fingers of my left hand, spreading her lips apart, exposing her clitoris. I gently slide my fingers of my right hand inside. Tight, really tight. She’s bleeding. I look up at her and ask, ‘Virgin?’ She’s crying and begging me to stop. Slowly I slide my pointer and middle finger of my right hand in and out the inside of her vagina. Slowly slide my pinky finger in her anus. I leaned down, lowering my head, my face into her Cooch. With my tongue I begin to flick her clitoris. Then I pull out my pointer and middle finger from her vagina, leaving my pinky finger in her ass.

“I lick from the taint up to the bottom of her vagina, up through, between the lips to the clitoris, like licking an ice-cream cone. She tastes incredible! I continue flicking her clitoris with my tongue. I slide my pointer finger slowly back in and out. Then with my pointer swooping from the inside left wall up to the top, across and down inside right wall, then back up, across, back down the left wall, then back, repeatedly back-and-forth and slowly sliding in and out at the same time, I continue flicking her clitoris with my tongue. I can tell she’s about to come. Her thighs are pulsating, as she’s twitching I continue flicking with my tongue and swooping my fingers side, up, over, side and back. She comes. Her orgasm is like a waterfall. My mouth is filled as her come drips down my chin. My right hand is soaked. I’ve never tasted anything so sweet, so bold before, so I dive back in, hoping she’ll come again.

“Angellous says, ‘Enough. Back to your wall!’

“I stand back up, off of her, lean away from the table, wipe my chin, then walk back to the far wall. I pick up the waist shack- le I was strapped in before. I open the shackle, wrap it around my waist, and re-lock it. I began to pace back and forth. I can’t sit. This hard-on really hurts. Angellous walks over to me. He hands me the camera and a memory card marked Saturday. Then he walks over to Callisto.

“Angellous says to Callisto, ‘I’ll remove the waist shackle, if you gonna.’

“Callisto interrupts and says, ‘Yes, yes, I’ll do what you want. Just don’t hurt me.’

“Angellous unlocks and removes Callisto’s waist shackle and he rebinds her wrists together. Then he grabs her left arm and pulls her sideways. He reaches behind her with his right hand while walking, grabbing her wrists that are bound behind her back. He walks her over, past the rack table and Marriessa, to this weird-looking seat that has a back board, straps, and a metal handle in the back of it. He turns her back to the seat of what he called, the Garrotte. He takes a step to her side and lifts her bound wrists up over the back post and sits her down. Walking around to the front of her, he reaches with his right hand to the left side of her head, and grazes her cheek with his fingers from front to back, reaching behind her head, and pulls a leather strap out around the front of her neck to the right side and behind. Then he turns his big handlebar in the back, turns it around, tightening the neck strap.

"Callisto says, 'Please?'

"Angellous kneels down in front of her, sliding his hands from the top of her knees up the sides of her thighs to the sides of her hips. He slides his fingers in the waistband of her black lace panties, sliding his fingers from the side to the front, to the back, lowering her panties down, down until they meet the seat of the Garrotte, back to the front, slowly pulling them down until they meet the top of her thighs.

"Callisto says, 'Please?'

"Angellous tugs her panties towards him, bringing her pant- ies out from behind the bottom, from where her butt meets the seat of the Garrotte, out to the beginning of her thighs. While looking up at her, he pulls her panties down her thighs, over her knees, and down to her ankles.

"Angellous says, 'Step out!'

"Callisto lifts her left leg, and Angellous pulls her black lace panties out from behind her ankle and down the bridge, off of her foot. Then she sets her left leg back down and her foot on the dirt floor. Then she raises her right leg, lifting her foot up off the floor. Angellous pulls her panties down around the back of her ankle, down the bridge, and off her foot. She sets her leg back down and her foot onto the dirt floor. He places her panties in his right, back pocket, then quickly spreads her knees apart with his hands.

“Angellous sits on the dirt floor and slides his feet between hers, along each side of the Garrotte. With her feet now on the outside of Angellous’s thighs, he slides his fingers up her shins to her knees, over the top of her knees and up her thighs, then stops. He pressed his elbows on the top of her knees and crossed his arms, then rested his chin on his wrist, staring up at her for about a half-hour. I don’t think their eyes ever left each other, and she never made a sound.

“Angellous lifts his head and uncrosses his arms. He places his hands on both sides of her perfect-toned ass and yanks her hips forward towards him, causing the leather strap to tighten around her neck. Then he tugs again. Now her but is barely sitting on the Garrotte, and she is wheezing, trying to breathe. Angellous takes his hands, slides them to the inside of her thighs, then under to the bottom of her thighs, and up under her butt. Then he lifts her a couple inches up, while staring up at her. He goes down on her. She must really taste great, the way he’s going to town, eating her.

“Callisto was moaning, ‘Yes, oh, yes, yes, oh, aha, a.’

“Callisto’s legs are buckling. While supporting her with his right hand, Angellous reaches into his left, back pocket and pulls out a knife. Callisto squeezes his head with her thighs, raising her knees. Angellous reaches up ‘n’ in with the knife. Callisto tenses up moaning, ‘Yes, oh, yes, yes, oh.’ Angellous digs in. Callisto’s body now relaxes. He lifts his head, with his chin and lips glistening with her cum, and a little blood dripping. (he must have cut her.) Angellous sets her back down and pulls his hands out from under her ass, then places his knife and hand on her left knee, supporting himself as he stands. She sits back up, relaxing the leather strap around her neck, allowing her to breathe freely. Callisto has this look on her face. Complete exhilaration and satisfaction. (erotic asphyxiation, good shit.)

“Angellous unzips his pants. Callisto turns her head. Angellous places his right hand on her head and turns her head back to face him. He removes his hand from her head and points the knife in her face. Then he drops the knife and unbuckles his belt, then undoes the button on his jeans, and slides his pants down just past his butt. Angellous lifts her head by her chin. He’s staring at her. He grabs a hold of his joystick with his left hand and starts to jerk off, staring into her face. About seven or eight minutes go by, and he cums on her face. Some drips down off of her cheek, down off of her chin, onto the top of her breast. Callisto never looked away. Angellous pulls his pants up and buttons, then zips up and re-buckles his belt as well.

“He picks up the knife from the dirt floor and walks over to the tool table, grabs a bag and a rag, and continues to walk over to the chest box. He opens it up and pulls her panties out from his back pocket and places them in the bag and drops the bag in the old chest box. He turns, walks to the tool table, grabs a towel, and walks back to Callisto. He wipes his cum off her face, neck, and chest. Then he walks back to the tool table, drops the towel, and rummages through the tools.

“He picks up this, I have no idea what it is. It has a handle and two chains with barbed wire tangled around each chain separately. (I’ll call it the shredder.)”

6
FOLLOW THROUGH

"Angellous walks over to Callisto with the shredder in his left hand, lays the barbed wire and tangled chains against the outside of her right thigh, and slowly he raises his hand, dragging the barbed wire chain up the outside of her thigh.

"Callisto screams, 'Ow.'

"He continues to raise it about two inches, maybe three, then he stops. Callisto was crying. He swings his arm out and away from her leg, pulling the barbed chain off of her.

"Angellous walks over to me, then leans down and unlocks the waist shackle from around my waist, stands back up, and hands me this Shredder. Then he points to Marriessa. We walk over to Marriessa laying on the rack table, still locked in the stabilizing restraint. Angellous, holding Marriessa's foot, turns her so her feet and hands are facing out to the side of the rack table towards us. He grabs me by the right elbow and pulls me in front of her and takes the shredder back, laying the barbed chain onto the outside of her left thigh.

"Angellous said, 'Finish what you start!'

"Then Angellous starts to drag the shredder across her thigh.

"Marriessa screams, 'Ow, stop please? Ow.'

"I told Angellous, 'Alright. Okay, I'll do it!'

"I take a hold of the handle of the shredder and I start to drag it across the outside of her left thigh. I feel horrible as she screams and cries of pain.

"Angellous laughs and says, 'Okay, that's not what I meant. But when you think she's had enough, put the shredder down and drop your pants.'

"I dropped the handle of the shredder, then I undid my pants and lowered them down past my butt cheeks. With my Wang in my hand, I slapped her face, her cheek, then try to slide it in her mouth, but she won't open, so I grab the Shredder that Angellous is holding on the table next to her thigh. I take the handle of the shredder from him and lift it up, dragging the barb chain onto her thigh. As she opens her mouth, yelling 'Ow.' I shove my throb- bing boner into her mouth. I let go of the shredder as Marriessa starts to suck on my dick, moving her head in and out, sliding her lips up and down the shaft of my dick, occasionally rolling her tongue around the head while sucking. (I come.) Marriessa tries to pull away. I hold her head still, until I finish. I continued hold- ing her head, keeping it in her mouth for another minute or two, waiting for her to finish swallowing, then I pulled out. Angellous takes the shredder away from me.

"I take a hold of her foot and spin her around, so her ass faces out off the rack table, grab a hold of her right shin and the top of her left shoulder as I slowly penetrate her dam near virgin vagina. (my god she's tight.) Slowly I thrust my hips, sliding my erection in and out. She is so tight. I've only been in her about a minute, but I'm about to come. I pull out, and force my din- gis deep in her ass. I start to come in her. I finish, pull out, and slide my willy back in her Cooch, now thrusting hard, my balls slamming against her right butt cheek. I hear the wet slapping. Marriessa came herself. About ten to fifteen minutes later, I feel it coming on again. I pull out, with my right hand, I grab her left shin and spin her to the right, bringing her head to the edge of the table. With both hands, I take a hold of her head. She won't open her mouth, so I slap her ass with my right hand. She opens to say, "ow," and I quickly stick my skin flute in her mouth. She's gagging and crying as I force her head down the shaft, deep in her throat now. She's puked on me. I let her back up until only the head is in her mouth, so she can catch her breath, then I force her head down, her mouth down the shaft of my dick again, deep down her throat. I'm coming; ah, ah, Marriessa's gagging. I pull halfway out, holding her head. She swallows. I stepped back and pulled up my pants.

"Angellous hands me a knife. I say, 'No, I won't!'

"Angellous says, 'Take it.'

"I dropped the knife on the floor. I start to unlock the stationary restraint that Marriessa is locked in.

"Callisto said, 'I'll do it!'

Angellous turns to her with a smile, walks over to the left side of Callisto, sitting on the Garrotte, unstraps the leather neck strap, grabs a hold of her bound wrist, raising her wrist up and over and off the backboard of the Garrotte as she stands up. Angellous walked Callisto over to me and the rack table and pointed to the waist shackle that's anchored to the wall. We walk over. Callisto locks the waist shackle around my waist, then walks back to Angellous and the rack table where Marriessa is laying and crying. Angellous picks up the knife off the dirt floor. Callisto turns her back to him, and he cuts the rope, releasing her bound wrists, freeing her hands, then places the knife back on the rack table.

"Angellous says, 'See the ropes, the knife, the leg irons!'

"Callisto kneels down, straps on the iron ankle shackle to her right leg, and stands up. She then turns to face Marriessa on the rack table, and unlatches the ankle locks of the stationary restraint. Callisto then pulls Marriessa's legs out of the restraint and rolls her on her back. She then extends Marriessa's left leg to the end of the table, reaches down, and pulls out and up a rope, strapping it around her left ankle. Then Callisto reaches up and grabs Marriessa's right leg, pulling and extending it down to the end of the table and reaches down, pulling up and out another rope and straps in her right ankle.

"Callisto reaches over top of Marriessa, taking a hold of the stationary restraint on each side of her and pulls the device apart, opening the device releasing her wrist. Callisto continues lifting up the stationary device out from around Marriessa's neck, completely releasing her from a stationary device. Callisto turns back to hand Angellous the stationary device. Angellous hands her back the knife. He then placed the stationary device on the floor to his right against a stone column. Callisto cuts the rope from around each of Marriessa's wrist. She takes a hold of Marriessa's hands and raises her arms above her head and ties each wrist separately with the rope at the top end of the table. Callisto then takes a step back, turns to the spoked wheel that's connected to the rack table, and slowly turns the wheel to tighten the rope, pulling Marriessa's body straight out on the rack table. Angellous walks to the tool table and grabs a mason jar and a squirt bottle. He then walks back to the rack table.

"Angellous says, 'Short and shallow, one-hundred cuts!'

"Callisto takes a knife, placing the edge of the blade on Marriessa's right-outside thigh. With a little pressure, Callisto pulls a knife backward toward herself, dragging the knife's edge down and into her skin, cutting Marriessa's thigh. She's only cut about two inches in length. Then she lifts up and out of her cut skin, raising the knife off her leg. Marriessa's screaming, crying, and begging Callisto to stop. Callisto moves the knife up a couple inches, drags the tip of the knife across the skin of the top of her thigh, and slides the edge of the blade between her thighs. Callisto turns the knife's edge into the skin of Marriessa's inside thigh and pulls up, cutting her again slowly, shallowly, in a smooth short cut. (This continued going on for a couple of hours.) The whole time, Marriessa's screaming, crying, begging in pain, exhaustively waiting for it to be over. Marriessa's now cut all over her arms, chest, breast, and stomach. The inside, top, and outside of her thighs are all cut up and bleeding as well.

"Angellous takes a couple steps to Callisto. Callisto is with her back against the rack table, facing Angellous. He takes the knife, leans to her right, and puts the knife on the table by Marriessa's elbows. Angellous places his hands on Callisto's hips and lifts her up on the rack table, sitting her on the edge of the table against Marriessa's bloody body. Angellous takes a hold of the shirt at the waist and lifts up off with his hands. He separates her closed knees as he steps in between her thighs and against her. He slides his fingers up her thighs, up the sides of her stomach, and up her ribs. He takes a hold of her halter top and lifts it up, pulls the front of her top out, and up over her B-size breasts. He slides his hand to the back, raising her shirt up to her shoulders. Callisto raises her arms straight over her head. Angellous lifts her shirt over her head. As Callisto lowers her arms back down, he then continues to pull her shirt off her arms.

"Angellous just stares for a minute, then he places his left hand on her right cheek of her face. He lowers his hand down her neck, over her right collarbone, and down her chest plate, between the top of her breast, over her heart. Softly holding her left arm, he pushes her to lean back on top of Marriessa's bleeding waist. Angellous is now fondling Callisto's breast, squeezing, and kissing, kissing her neck, lips, to earlobes, down her neck, collarbone, her breast. While kissing down her mid-drift to her bellybutton, Angellous stares up at her. Callisto is arching her back and lowering her hips, with her right hand holding Angellous's head and with her left hand clawing at the table as Angellous went down on her.

"A few minutes later Angellous raises his head, his cheeks 'n' chin glistening and dripping. Callisto exhales into a physical-relaxed state. Callisto sits up and reaches for Angellous's belt. She unbuckles his belt, unbuttons and unzips his pants. Together they lower his pants down to his knees. Callisto, with her left hand, grabs a hold of Angellous's love torpedo and pulls him in close to her, as she lowers his head down over her clitoris, allowing the helmet to graze and push her lips wide, forcing his head into the opening of her vagina. Angellous, with his left hand on her right breast, his right hand on her left side, lowers Callisto back down, down even more than the last time.

"Now laying on top of Marriessa's blood-covered waist, Marriessa still crying, bound to the rack table, unable to move and bleeding even more every time her skin is moved, Callisto is breathing heavily and rolling her hips up and down, forward and backwards. Angellous is thrusting in and out, while rolling his hips up and down, in and out, side to side, up, in, down, out, up. He is now slowing down. Callisto is really panting. Angellous leans in and lays his head on her chest plate. Exhausted, Callisto lays her head back onto Marriessa's stomach and holds Angellous's left arm with her right hand, with her left hand, she held the back of his head.

"After a few minutes goes by, Angellous stands up. He pulls his dong out, leans down, and pulls up his pants. He helps Callisto off the table by holding her hand. Angellous steps to the end of the rack table, picks up a Mason jar, opens the lid, and hands it to Callisto, then rubs his fingers together, waving his hand over Marriessa's body. Callisto dips her fingers into the jar and pulls out her fingers, sprinkling this powder over Marriessa's right thigh. Marriessa's torso lunges up off the table. As she screams in severe pain, the skin on Marriessa's right thigh is bubbling. Callisto steps back. She has this look of horror on her face.

"Angellous laughs and says, 'Powder chemical called lye.'

"Callisto dips her fingers again into the Mason jar, pulling her fingers out, spreading some more lye over Marriessa's left thigh, then on her stomach. Angellous grabs Callisto's hand as she is about to sprinkle on Marriessa's breast, stopping her. He walked around to the left of Callisto. He grabs the knife laying on the table by Marriessa's elbows and cuts Marriessa's inside-right breast, up and over the top. Marriessa, screaming, finally passes out from the pain. Angellous leans in and over Marriessa and licks the blood from her breast where he just cut. He stands back up, blood dripping from his chin, and turns, grabs Callisto by the base of her head, and pulls her to him. He kisses her deeply with his blood-soaked lips and chin.

"Angellous lets go of Callisto's head, taking her by her arm, walks her to the head of the rack table. Angellous walks to the other end, unstraps Marriessa's right leg, and lifts her foot up and over her head by her wrist. He reaches down below the table and pulls up this chain and wraps it over and around her right ankle. Then he walks around to the other side of the table and unties her left leg, lifting her foot up over her head by her other wrist. He reaches down again, taking a hold of the chain, and pulls up, wrapping the other end of the chain around Marriessa's left ankle, leaving Marriessa folded in half with her feet up by her hands at the top corners of the table.

"Angellous walks to the tool table and picks up a bottle of vinegar. He walks back over to the rack table where Marriessa is folded over in chains, her skin still bubbling. Angellous opens the bottle of vinegar and dumps it all over Marriessa's legs, ass, and stomach, stopping the chemical burn. Then he climbed up and knelt on the table. Unbuckles his belt, then his pants-button, unzips, and drops his pants to his knees. He crawls up on top of Marriessa. He reaches up between her thighs, her knees, and slaps her. He slaps her again, this time harder than the first. As Marriessa wakes crying and in excruciating pain, Angellous reaches up, takes a hold of Callisto's head, and pulls her down to Marriessa's face.

"Angellous says, 'Kiss!'

"Callisto starts kissing Marriessa's lips and fondling her breast. Angellous lifts himself up with his left hand as he slides his peter inside, violating Marriessa, my, Marriessa. He slammed himself into her, harder and harder in between the kisses from Callisto.

"Marriessa is crying and saying, 'Ow, stop. Ow, ow, please?' "Angellous just thrusts harder, putting his whole body into the thrust, into 'n' up inside my Marriessa. Angellous stops, waits a minute, then lifts up and pulls out of Marriessa. Angellous's cornholer is bloody and brown goo-covered. He had anal sex and tore her part. Callisto stands up, walks to the tool table, and grabs a rag. She walks back to the rack table, back to Angellous. She wipes the blood and shit off his weiner. Dips the rag in a bucket of water that is sitting at the end of the table. Soaking the rag, she turns back to Angellous and finishes washing him off, washing until he's clean. Now he is sitting on the edge of the table, and Callisto goes down on him, sucking his tallywacker. He comes. She swallows as she looks up. Then she stands up. Angellous hops off the table, and Callisto pulls up his pants, zips him up, and buttons up the pants, then re-buckles his belt.

"Angellous takes Callisto by the hand and walks over to the small door where he pulled out the barrel of water before. As he bent down and open the door, he pointed. Callisto, holding the wall above the door with her right hand, reaches in and pulls out a barbecue. Callisto picks up the one end and drags it out to the center of the room. Angellous walks over to Marriessa on the rack table, unchains her left ankle, then lowers her leg back down. He re-ties her ankle at the bottom end of the table. He walks back up to her torso, (the middle of the rack table) picks up the knife, and cuts into her left breast. He's cutting the skin off her left breast. Marriessa is screaming and she's bleeding a lot.

"With her left breast now completely skinned, Angellous lifts her breast muscle up, slides the knife up to the bottom of her breast against her rib cage, and slowly cuts her breast muscle off her body, from the bottom to the top. Marriessa passes out from the pain. Angellous lays the breast on the table and cuts it in half. Hands both pieces to Callisto, to cook on the barbecue. Walks to the tool table and picks up the fireplace shovel. Then walks over to Callisto. He sticks the iron shovel in the barbecue, a couple minutes. He flips her breast muscle over on the grill and pulls out the iron shovel from the fiery coals.

"The flat iron was glowing orange. He walked back to Marriessa on the rack table and applied a flat side of the iron shovel to her body where her left tit used to be, searing her skin to stop the bleeding. Marriessa wakes screaming and flopping on the table. Angellous peels the iron shovel off her. It's as if it was melted to her body. He only held it for a few seconds. Angellous sets the iron shovel down on the table alongside Marriessa and walks back to Callisto and the Bar-B-Q, shuts off the gas, and pulls out a flat tray. Sticks a knife in one-half of her breast, lifting it up off the barbecue, and drops it on the tray, then the second piece of her breast. Angellous cuts it up into small pieces. Callisto and Angellous feed each other what used to be Marriessa's left side of her great rack.

"Angellous and Callisto finished eating. Angellous then kiss- es Callisto and turns. He walks out of the room and down the hallway. We hear the floor door close. I'm trying to talk Callisto into letting us go. She's ignoring me. A day or two go by. We hear the door opening. It's Angellous. He's coming down the hall to the room. I can hear him mumbling. I see him now. He's entering the room. He looks furious. I watch him as he slams this contain- er on the tool table.

"Callisto says, 'What's wrong Huny?'

"'Graham, Lieutenant; W. Graham. Fucking cop!!'

"Callisto turns Angellous to face her and kisses him hello. Angellous turns back to the table, picks up a saw and a knife, hands Callisto the knife, points to Marriessa.

"Angellous says, 'Lunch' as he points to Marriessa.

"She walked over to Marriessa laying on the rack table. Angellous points to Marriessa's right breast.

"Marriessa is begging Callisto, 'No, please no. Kill me; please, just kill me!'

"Callisto grabs Marriessa's right calf, unwraps the chain that's wrapped around her right ankle, raises her leg up over and back down to the table, extending her leg straight out, and hands Marriessa's ankle to Angellous at the end of the table. He re-tied her ankle to the table. Callisto, with her left hand, grabs Marriessa's right breast, squeezes, and pulls up. Angellous walks behind Callisto, takes a hold of her right hand holding the knife. Together they cut into Marriessa's last breast, slowly peeling back the skin of her tit as they cut her skin away from her breast. Marriessa screams this ungodly scream. Callisto grabs her boozum muscle, squeezes, and pulls up, placing the blade at the bottom of her breasts against her ribs, cutting up against her rib cage, slowly removing her right boob. Marriessa passes out once again from the pain.

"Callisto lays the muscle on the table and cuts it in half, picks up both pieces, and walks around over to the barbecue and places them on the grill, cooking what used to be a right breast. Angellous, walks to the tool table a picks up a saw, turns and walks back to the rack-table. He starts cutting into Marriessa like she's an animal, starting first with her leg. Callisto flips the two pieces of meat. (her right breast.) He cuts down into her skin, muscle, into and through her femur mussel, down further into and through the bone, down into the muscle, skin, completely cutting her right leg off.

"Callisto says, 'Lunch!'

"Angellous stops cutting. Walks around the table and over to Callisto. As she is cutting up the breast muscle, Angellous tosses me half of the right breast, and Callisto begins eating the other.

"Angellous says, 'When done eating. Her leg, same cut. Then at her shoulders the left then the right. Careful, it's a little difficult separating the arm from the shoulder. Roll her over, her gluteus, each butt cheek a good roast.'

"While Callisto is sawing Marriessa's limbs off, Angellous cuts a slab of muscle from Marriessa's legs and throws it on the grill, cooking it. When it was finished, he gave it to me, a little piece of her leg muscle, which he cooked medium rare. I haven't eaten in a week at least. So I ate both of the cooked muscle's. It taste like an Angus Steak. Angellous walks back to the rack table. Shows Callisto how to De-bone meat. Piece by piece she cuts, cutting the skin off the muscle, then cutting away Marriessa's muscles from the bone.

"Both of them are now covered in blood. Angellous undoes the buckle and drops his pants, then slams Callisto's face into the rack table. As he takes her from behind, she moans. Angellous finishes. Placing his forehead on her back, he steps back, reaches down, and pulls out of her. She turns around, grabs a hold of his trouser snake. Angellous slides the muscles to the side of the table, hops up on the table. Callisto kneels down and begins jerking him off, staring up at him. Takes a hold of Callisto by her shoulders and lifts her up, over the table above him. Callisto straddles over and then places the tip of his beef bazooka in her pussy and sits down into his lap. She's rolling her hips, raising herself up and down. Angellous is fondling her breast, and they are kissing each other as she rides him. Angellous pulls her in closer to him. With his hands on her back, breathing heavy. As she slows to stop, she just sits there with him inside her. Callisto finally gets up, sweaty and bloody, and climbs off him and down off the table. Angellous hops down, and Callisto pulls up his pants, buttons, and zips, then buckles his belt.

"Angellous walks to the tool table, grabs a container, and walks to the rack table and puts the muscles from Marriessa's body into the container. He pulls out a burlap cloth sack and puts the bones of Marriessa's body in it. Angellous squats down and removes the shackle from Callisto's right ankle. He stands up and picks up the container and hands it to Callisto. He then grabs the burlap sack of bones. They both walk out the room and down the hallway. I hear the door close. A couple minutes go by. I could hear the pigs grunting, snorting in a frenzy."

***

Back at the bar, Kasey Jones pub & grub

The five small-town cops, are all listening tentatively, as if holding onto every last word, eager to hear the next.

7
LT. W. GRAHAM

"Angellous and Callisto have been gone for what seems to be days. I was left chained to a stone wall. The blood on the rack table from Marriessa's body is still moist. The blood that dripped off the table has stained the dirt floor a rust color.

"The door, I can hear it opening. It's Callisto. As she walked in, I noticed she's covered in blood.

I ask her, 'Unlock me before he comes.'

"She walks over to me, tries to unlock the ankle shackle, but it won't unlock. Footsteps. Callisto jumps up and walks over to the water barrel. Picks up a bucket and dips the bucket into the barrel, filling the bucket with water. She lifts it up and out, turns, walks back over to the rack table.

"Angellous walks in, dragging these two cops by a belt wrapped around their feet 'n' ankles. He lets go of the belt, drop- ping the cop's legs to the floor. Angellous walks to the tool table, to the battery charger, and turns it on. Throws the cables at Callisto's feet. Callisto shakes violently. Angellous shuts off the battery charger, and Callisto drops to the floor. She's laying on the blood-soaked dirt floor, passed out. Angellous turns to the table and puts a tape in the player. (Lynyrd Skynrd, "Free Bird") Angellous leans down, picking up one of the belts that is tied to the cop's foot, dragging the one cop to the chair that Callisto was first on. He grabs a hold of the cop by his hair, pulls him back- wards and up into the chair, strapping his waist from behind, then walks around to face the cop. He leans down and straps the cop's right wrist, then the left wrist, to the arms of the chair. Angellous squats down and straps the cop's legs, at the bottom of his shins, to the legs of the chair. Then he stands up and backhands the cop. That really had to hurt, dam-near knocked the cop's head off.

"He walks back over to the second cop, then leans down, picks up the belt that's wrapped around his feet, drags him to the little holding room, that I was once in. Grabbing the cops head he shoves the cop into the little room, ripping out a chunk of his hair. As Angellous closes the holding room door, he looks down into his hand and laughs at the chunk of hair, then stuffs it into his pocket.

"Callisto is moving but not getting up. Angellous walks to the grill and lights it up. Walks back around the rack table, over to Callisto and helps her to her feet.

"Callisto says, 'I'm sorry!'

"She leans in to hold Angellous as he caress Callisto's long black silky curly hair.

"Angellous says, 'On the shelf above the tool table, get the iron branding rods and lay them on the grill!'

"Before she can move, he grabs her arm with his left hand. He lifts her head by her chin and kisses her. As Callisto walks away, he lets go of her arm. She continues to walk over to the tool table. Angellous walks out of the room and down the hall. Callisto grabs the iron branding rods, walks to the barbecue, places the branding end of the rods on the grill. She walks over to the front of the cop that's strapped to the chair, rips the buttoned up uniform shirt open, showing his bare chest.

"Angellous walks in with a plastic bag. Setting it down on

the tool table, pulls plastic containers out of the bag. With one container and a bottle of water, he walks over and hands them to me. (It's Food) Beef and broccoli with gravy, Nice.

"Angellous walks over to Callisto by the cop. He pulls out a knife and walks behind the cop. With his left hand, he grabs the cop's hair on the top of his head and pushes his head forward and down. With the knife in his right hand, he carves a symbol into the back of the cop's neck. We can see the cop is in pain, but he dared not say a word. Angellous yanks the cop's head back. Then walks around to the front of the cop, next to Callisto, and hands her the knife. He points to the cop. Then he turns and walked to the stock in the far corner, next to me, and leans against it watching.

"Callisto begins cutting the cop, short and shallow cuts. The cop tried not to scream. This continued for a good half-hour. She must have cut him at least forty times. Callisto seems to have lost interest. She turns, walking past the rack table, and sets down the knife on the tool table. She picked up this plastic bag, lifted it up shoulder-height and smiled at Angellous. She turned around, walked back to the cop.

Callisto says, 'Don't want to scream. Salt; for good measure.'

"She reached deep in the plastic bag, pulled out a hand full of this granule powder, then rubbed it into the forty some-odd cuts. He screamed this painfully-felt scream. She laughed, turned towards us, walked over to Angellous by the stocks and begins to strip him.

"He sits Callisto down on the bench behind the stock and leans her back. He opens the stock, places her forearms in the cut-outs, then raises her legs up over her torso, places her feet through the cut-outs of the stock, then closes it, locking her ankles and arms in place. It must be awkward. Her legs are pulled out straight, alongside her arms. He gently pulls her head back, laying the base of her head on the stock. He pushes her forehead back further, extending her neck, and pulls this metal bar over her neck and locks it in place on the other side. He walks around the stock to the bench. He slaps her ass. He slaps the lips of her pussy until red and swollen. Angellous sits on the bench. He leans his head in and starts licking the lips of her vagina. She's moaning, his left hand playing with her lips, and he smacks her ass, with his right hand, he has his left pointer and middle finger in her pussy and his thumb in her ass, pushing them in and out as Callisto is moaning, 'More, more.'

"Angellous stands up, unbuttons, and drops his pants. Pulling one pant leg off, he stands over her and pushes his ding-a- ling straight down, lowering himself into her (tea bag) up and down, raising himself in and out, squashing his balls against her. He stopped and pulled out.

"He stepped a couple of inches back, then up on to the bench, leaned over her, placing his hands down on the stock, on each side of her head, slowly forcing his timber in her ass, in and out, slow turned to rough. She's tearing in pleasure and grunting in pain. She's bleeding. He pulls out and climbs off by stepping down. He walks around by her head. He pushes her head down toward the floor, completely extending her neck and opening her mouth. He slides his shit-covered meat stick in her mouth, in and out. I watch as I see her throat expanding and contracting. He forces himself all the way down into her throat. Her throat is expanding at her collarbone as she is choking. Angellous begins to moan in release, 'Ah ha AA AA' he came and pulled out. She's smiling. Angellous pulls up his pants, buttons them, and walks away, leaving her in the stocks.

"Angellous walks over to the cop strapped to that chair with his arms and his chest bleeding. With his right fist, Angellous punches the cop square in the face. He yelled, 'Pull Me Over?' Then he punches him with his left fist and said,

‘For what?’ Angellous punches the cop again and again with his right fist.

“The cop said, ‘Was just a routine stop!’

“Angellous replied, ‘Routine.’

“Walks over to the grill and picks up one of the three branding rods that have been burning on the barbecue. He walks back in front of the cop with the amber-glowing hot, iron branding rod in his right hand.

“The cop’s spitting blood as he says, ‘Please no, no.’

“As Angellous presses the end of the amber-glowing branding iron into the cop’s bicep, burning through his shirt and skin, I see the cop is tensed up and he is trying to take the pain. Then yells, ‘NO.’ Angellous stops, walks over to Callisto, pulls the pins out, opening the neck collar of the stock, then lifts her head up and opens the stock, releasing her legs and arms. Angellous steps to the side, bends down, and picks up her clothes, then hands them to her. She starts to get dressed. He drops his pants around his ankles and shimmies up to her. He stands between her legs, between her thighs. He reaches down, taking a hold of the sides of each of her breasts with his hands. He shimmies forward again and starts to jerk himself off with her breast. As Angellous is about to come, Callisto goes down on him, sucking his dick. She swallows. They finish. Angellous steps back and watches Callisto as she finishes getting dressed. He takes Callisto by the hand, and they walk back over to the cop.

“Callisto says, ‘W. Graham. What’s that stand for? Wuss!’

“The cop garbles, ‘William.’

“She laughs, turns to Angellous. Stepped up against him, and they begin kissing. She takes the knife out from his back pocket while they are kissing. She stops, turned to the tool table, and picked up a pair of pliers, turned back to the cop, stabs through his right arm into the chair with the knife. The cop opens his mouth, screams 'Ow.' Callisto takes the pliers in her right hand and grabs the cop's tongue, squeezes, and pulls his tongue out of his mouth. With her left hand she takes the knife still in his arm. She wiggles it forward and backward yanking the knife up and out of the cop's arm. She places the edge of the blade on the top of the cop's tongue as he fidgets, mumbling, begging her no. She slowly cuts side to side, slicing through his tongue. Back and forth until his tongue comes off. She then hands back the knife to Angellous and takes the tongue out of the pliers and tosses it over onto the grill. Turns back to Angellous, smiling, then walks to the tool table. She puts the pliers back. She squats down, picking up the cables to the battery charger. She reaches over and turns the battery charger on, sets the level to four. (Nine-hundred WATTS) Battery charger cable clamps no longer have the sponges in their teeth.

"Holding the battery charger cables, she walks over to the cop. She squeezes the negative cable clamp with her right hand. She squeezes the handle, opening the clamp teeth. She looks in the cop's face with a smile and shoves the open clamp up be- tween his legs, then releases the clamp handle. The teeth of the clamp is firmly biting into his pants. By the sound of his screaming, I'd say the clamp was on his balls or his dick. Callisto then dropped the other clamp, the positive cable, on the cop's shoulder, electrocuting him. The cop is jolting and bouncing around as the positive cable clamp slowly falls down his chest to his hip. The cop can't even scream. With his body locked up, the positive clamp falls off his hip to the side of the chair and onto the floor. "Angellous shuts off the battery charger and yanks the cables back, ripping the negative cable off of the cop's family jewels, taring the crotch of his pants. The cop who is now, thankfully passed out is bleeding from where the clamp was attached to his shit. He's bleeding pretty badly. The blood is already dripping down the chair. Angellous and Callisto walked out of the room and down the hall. I can hear the door close.

"About a day goes by. I hear the door opening. I'm just sitting against the wall. I can't get out, so why fight. They're coming down the hall into the room. I hear Angellous and Callisto talking and laughing.

"Angellous asks Callisto, 'Hey, where is the other one's badge?'

"Callisto says, 'At the foot of the couch, in the Henderson's house!'

"Holding-room cop says, 'Henderson's? What did you two do?'

"Callisto laughs, as Angellous replies, 'Pinned a double homicide on your badge.' Then he continued going on to say, 'Oh and I carved my symbol in the back of their necks for you. It's just like the carving on your partner's neck.'

"Holding-room cop said, 'You won't get away with this! Let us go, and confess. Maybe then, if you're lucky, they won't give you the death penalty!'

"Angellous giggles, 'That makes thirteen families linked to you!'

"Lieutenant; Graham tries to talk, but all you hear is, 'Um ma oh am.'

"Angellous, standing by the table, laughs hysterically at Lieutenant; Graham. He tells Callisto to lower the wall chain. Callisto walks over to the column and unhooks it, releasing the chain from the column, raising the chain, lowering the other end with the hook to the floor. Angellous walked over to Lieutenant; Graham in the chair, squats down, and cuts the cop's pants, pulling them free from his waist and legs. He throws the cut-up pants to the side, pulls out his knife from his back pocket, and places the blade between the ankle bone and ankle tendon, shoving the tip of the blade through his skin, muscle and out the other side. Lieutenant; Graham screams. Angellous looks up with a smile and yanks the knife, pulling it out of his left ankle, then slowly shoves the tip of the blade through his right ankle.

"Angellous tells Callisto, 'Bring me the hanger! It's a triangle-shaped piece of iron with a hook at two ends.'

"Callisto goes to the tool table, rummages a little. She found it. I can only imagine what they're gonna do. She brings the hang- er over to Angellous. Angellous takes the hanger from Callisto, shoves the hook on one side of the triangle hanger through the cut in the cop's right ankle, then forces the second hook on the other side of the hangar triangle into his left ankle. Lieutenant; Graham is just screaming in agony.

"Angellous unstraps his legs from the legs of the chair, grabs the point of the hanger, and lifts up. Graham screams. Angellous, holding the tip of the hanger, reaches over and unstraps Grahams waist from the chair, then unstraps both of his arms. Angellous drags the Lieutenant off the chair onto the dirt floor by the hang- er in his ankles. He continues to drag him over to the raising chain. He leans down, picks up the hook off the dirt floor, and latches it onto the point of the hanger. Graham tries vigorously to pull away. Angellous walks to the column by Callisto and pulls the chain down, click. click. click. click. click. click, slowly, yet steadily dragging Graham back and up, hanging him from his ankles. Hanging him, so his fingers barely scrape the dirt floor. Angellous and Callisto look at each other and walk out, holding each other around each other's waist.

"I asked the other cop in the holding room, 'What's your name?'

"'Sargent; David Campbell! It was a routine stop. He was acting abrupt. So we told him to get out the truck. I was running their names. You know, wants and warrants. She was clean. Next thing I know, Graham was face down in the street and the girl had a gun in my face. Then I heard it.

Dispatcher said, 'Person wanted for questioning in a multiple murders, a kidnapping of one Marriessa, age seventeen His- panic, approximately five foot two inches, one-hundred and five pounds black hair. Last seen at the gas and go on Route 80 west. If you have any information on the whereabouts of a red shitty ford pickup, do not approach. Call your local Sheriff. Believed to be armed and dangerous. Repeat. Do not approach! Wanted for questioning in multiple murders and kidnapping. Any information on the location of this vehicle and any occupants should be reported to your local Sheriff.'

"She must have hit me on the head, cause the next thing I know, I'm waking up in the back of a red truck, hog tied and gagged. I tried struggling free, then I wake up here. How long have you been here?'

"'I don't know. Three maybe four months, maybe more. Do what they say. Shh shh, they're coming! Trust me. Just keep quiet.'

"Angellous and Callisto walked back in with another plas- tic tote box. Callisto walks over and lights the grill. Angellous reaches into the tote and pulls out two big slabs of meat. He then walks the slabs over to Callisto and lays them each on the grill. Angellous then handed her another knife and points to Lieu- tenant; Graham, the cop hanging upside down.

"Angellous says, 'His manhood, a waste!'

"Callisto smiles as she walks over to Lieutenant; Graham. With her left hand, Callisto takes a hold of his dick and balls. With the knife in her right hand, she places the edge of the blade at the bottom of his sack, the beginning of the taint, pulling his wankie and his family jewels out from his body, then slowly cutting his ball sack, slicing back and forth, rocking the blade side to side, until he is completely castrated (She cut his manhood off.) Angellous walks over with a red-hot branding iron and shoves it into what once was his crotch. The whole time, Lieutenant; Graham is bellowing this ungodly scream.

"Angellous points and says, 'Grill.'

"Callisto walks over to the grill with Grahams family jewels in her hand, dripping with blood, then lays them on the grill. Graham passed out from the pain. Angellous walks over to the grill and Callisto. With a single swoop, he scoops up Grahams manhood (dick and balls) off the grill and walks over to the holding room. He squats down, unlocks the little door, lays Grahams manhood on the dirt floor, then closes and re-locks the little door.

"Angellous says to Campbell, 'Eat or starve.'

"Angellous walks back over to Callisto, grabs her hand, and walks her to the barrel, washes her hands off, then starts taking her clothes off piece by piece. He lifts up and pulls off her halter top and slides her skirt down to the dirt floor as she steps out. Then he kneels down, reaching up to take a hold of her black lace panties, and slides them down past her thighs, her knees, off her legs, as she steps up and out. He wet sponged her entire body. Then he walks her a couple steps backwards, presses her up against the stone wall.

"He gets on his knees. She raises her right leg to the side of his head. He kisses inside the thigh and cuts her short and shallow. Grabs a hold of her leg, with both hands on the outside of her thigh, as she leans back into the stone wall. I can see him swallowing. She's grabbing her right breast with her right hand and fingering herself with her left hand. (God damn that's hot.) Angellous is still drinking. Callisto's about to come. She grabs a hold of Angellous head with her left hand, shoves his face in her pussy. She comes. He's rolling his head in and out as if to take it all in. Angellous pulls his head away, reaches back and over to the grill, and flips both slabs a meat.

"He turns back to Callisto, lifts up her leg as he stands up. She unzips his pants and pulls out his meat thermometer, puts him in her. He starts thrusting up and in, out and down, harder and harder each time he thrusts back in. He stopped, pulled out. Takes her by the hair of her head, steps to the side, and pushes her head toward the floor, bending her over. With her hands on the dirt floor, he steps behind, between her legs. Reaches down to the outside of her thighs, taking a hold of her legs, lifting her legs up to his waist, looks like a wheel-barrel. She reaches up and puts him back inside her. He begins thrusting again. He drops to his knees, sets her legs down one leg at a time, for her to be on her knees, and they continue about twenty minutes. He must of got off. He didn't make a sound, but he must have, because he stopped. He stands back up, pulls up his pants, then walks over to the barrel and grabs the sponge out from the water and hands it to Callisto. As Angellous turns back to the grill, Callisto was washing the dirt off her.

"Angellous takes the meat off the grill, lays it on a metal sheet, and begins to cut up the slabs of meat. Callisto finishes washing, walks to Angellous, takes a piece of meat with her fingers, and feeds it to Angellous. She reaches back down and picks up the other slab of meat and walks over to me. I asked her for another piece. Intern; she slaps me in the face and walks back to Angellous. I eat and watch as they bickered with each other.

"I hear moaning. Graham is waking up."

8
ACCOMPLICE

"Angellous and Callisto finished bickering. Callisto brings me the last piece of meat. Angellous goes around picking up all three buckets, (our toilet buckets) and walks out of the room and on down the hallway. A few minutes go by. Callisto occupied her time by straightening up the tool table. Angellous comes back in the room with the three buckets and a cork-board. He places the cork-board by the tool table, the first bucket by the far wall, second bucket next to me, and the third he placed outside the holding room, where Sargent; David Campbell is locked in.

"Angellous walks over to the cork-board, picks it up, and walks over to the first wall, the wall to the right coming into the room from the hallway. Callisto walks over to Angellous with a brown lunch bag and hands it to Angellous. She then walked back to the tool table, pulled out a one-gallon, metal container of turpentine, and started cleaning the tools, as Angellous opens the brown lunch bag and pulls out pictures, pinning the pictures one by one on the cork board. Pictures were faraway. I couldn't really see them that good. It looks like all the pictures are of dead people. Angellous finishes hanging the last picture, stands up, looks to his left, looking to the holding room.

Angellous says, "Campbell. You do remarkable work!"

Campbell replies, "You sick Fuck! You killed all those people?"

"Your badge, your partner's fingerprints, oh, and your DNA." "Angellous and Callisto began giggling, like demented children.

Campbell continues to say, "You'll never get away with it!" "Angellous walks over to Lieutenant; Graham who is hanging. Tells Callisto to bring in the hatchet and torch. Callisto searches for the hatchet in the mess of tools laying on the tool table. She found it, I can see it in her hands. She walks over to Angellous and hands it to him. Angellous, with a hatchet in his right hand, grabs Lieutenant; Grahams left forearm, pulls his arm up and out in front of him. Callisto walks to the wall by the tool table and grabbed the torch, while Angellous began hacking, just hacking away. It must of took six or seven times to cut off Grahams left hand at the wrist with the hatchet.

"Callisto starts to walk back to Angellous as Grahams hand falls to the dirt floor. Angellous turned back and hands Callisto the hatchet, takes the torch. Graham is screaming and flailing around. Angellous lights the torch and presses the tip of the flame onto his wrist, burning, searing closed his hacked up wrist where his hand used to be. Angellous turns again and hands the torch back to Callisto. He bends down and picks up the severed hand, tosses it on the rack table. Callisto, holding the torch, walks back to the wall by the tool table, shuts the torch off, and puts it back in its holder. She walked in front of the table.

Angellous says, "Fillet knife please,"

Callisto says, "This one?" As she is holding up a butcher knife.

Angellous replied, "No, it's a quarter the thickness of that butcher knife you're holding."

"Callisto's rummaging through the massive mass of tools. She yells, "I found it!" Quickly she turned around and walks over to Graham, who is still hanging. She hands Angellous the fillet knife.

Angellous, holding Graham by his arms, says, "Take a hold of his forearms, pull them up in front of him and around past his hips towards you, so they're behind him, then pull down to the floor."

"Callisto's in front of Graham with his arm hanging toward the floor. She takes a hold of Grahams right arm, lifts his arm out in front of him, then up towards his waist. She walks around to the back of him. She reaches down and grabs Grahams hand-less left arm, lifts it up and out, in front of him, up to his waist, with both of his forearms against his waist. She starts pulling back and down, pulling his forearms down towards her, away from his back, forcing them backwards towards the floor.

"Angellous takes the knife, cuts the skin around Grahams left ankle, cuts straight down the whole length of the inside of his leg. He reaches back up to Grahams right ankle and cuts around his ankle as he did with the left leg. Angellous cuts the whole length of the inside of his right leg from ankle bone down to his u-nick crotch. The whole time Graham is flailing and bouncing around, screaming in agonizing, excruciating pain. Angellous reaches back up to Grahams ankles, takes the fillet knife, cuts in behind the skin, and slowly peels down, cutting the skin off Grahams left leg.

"Even with all that blood rushing to his head, while all this time hanging upside down, he is still screaming and bouncing around from the pain of being skinned alive.

"Angellous, working his way down and around inch by inch, peeling in cutting, peeling, cutting the skin off of Grahams left leg. Now he's down at the hip. The skin from his left leg is just hanging down against Grahams torso. All of the left leg muscles are exposed. Angellous starts on Grahams right leg, back up to the ankle, cuts in, and starts peeling inch-by-inch, cutting, peeling back the skin off of Grahams right leg. Inch-by-inch, all the way down to his hips, letting the skin from his right leg hang down against his torso, like his left. Graham wiggling, the skin from his legs keeps bouncing off his chest, smacking him in the face. Both legs and glut's are now fully exposed. There is no skin left on either of the legs, only bare muscles.

"Angellous takes a hold of the skin from the left leg and cuts it free from Grahams hip, then reaches around and cuts the skin of Grahams right leg, cuts it off at the hip as well. With both pieces of skin, Angellous walks to the rack table, lays the skin out, with the inside of the skin facing up and the outside of the skin facing down on the table. He walks over to the end of the rack table, reaches down in a bag, and pulls out a cup. He stands back up, turns, and takes a couple steps back to the center of the rack table. With the cup in his left hand, he sprinkles this white powder-looking stuff, covering the skin. Angellous sets down the cup, walks back to the tool table. He picks up a Shaffer and a grill fork, then walks back to the rack table, stabs the grill fork through the skin into the table with his left hand. With his right holding the Shaffer, he drags it across the skin three times, from fork to hip. He picks up the cup again, turns and walks back to the bag, dips the cup back down in the bag at the foot of the table, walks back to the center, and sprinkles the white stuff again over the skin. It must be salt. He pulls out the grill fork, out of the table, out of the skin, stabs through the second piece of leg skin, through the skin into the table. He refills the cup and sprinkles, what I think is salt, on the second skin, then shaffers the skin three times, like he did with the first skin. Once again he sprinkles the salt. Angellous sets down the Shaffer and the cup, walks over to the chair, and sits down. Callisto is just staring at Lieutenant; Grahams skinless legs.

I said to Angellous, "Cops? You know, they gonna give you the death penalty."

Angellous replied, "Nope, not me!" With a big smile.

"Callisto looks at me, then Angellous. She looks back at Graham, walks over to Angellous, and squats down onto her knees, unzips Angellous's pants. She has her right hand on his left leg by his hip. Her left hand is holding his third leg. She began licking, then lipping the head of his weeny. As he gets hard, she slides his love muscle in her mouth, her lips over his head, down his shaft, back up, rolling her tongue around his head while looking up at him, then slides her lips down his shaft again. Angellous leans his head back. Callisto is rolling her head as she slides her lips up and down his little man, with her cheeks of her face sucked in. Angellous grips the arms of the chair. (That must be one hell of a blow job.) Callisto reaches up with her right hand and drags her nails down his chest, while looking up at him. Angellous lowers his head and looks down at her.

Angellous said, "Don't stop, don't stop, stop. Ah, ha aah."

"Callisto swallows every last drop and continues going down on him, sliding her lips down the shaft of his dick. Angellous grabs her shoulders and pulls her up. Callisto straddles Angellous, reaches down with a smile on her face, and puts the head of his meat piston in between her lips. She slowly tries to sit down on him, into his lap, allowing him up inside her. She rises and lowers, rises and lowers all the way down into his lap. She begins moaning as she is raising up and slamming down rapidly. Hearts pumping, endorphins multiplying, she raises up, then lowers down while rolling her hips. She's moaning, "Ah ha AA Ah Aah." Angellous, with his right hand, takes a hold and supports the small of her back. With his left hand, he grips her right breast. As Callisto leans back and claws down Angellous's neck and chest, Callisto gets louder, "Yes, yes, yes." Then slows to a stop, leans in, and kisses him. Angellous, still in her, leans his head back, falls asleep, Callisto rest her head on his collarbone and fell asleep as well. That is one really great Orgasm that Callisto had! "Callisto. Callisto. Get up Callisto. Strap him in!" I whispered.

"Callisto wakes up. She leans up, looking at Angellous, turns her head, and looks at me, smiles as she looks down into their lap. Callisto, slowly, softly starts kissing Angellous' neck and chest, his ear, neck, rolling her hips ever so slightly. Angellous awakes smiling. He raises his left hand, sliding up her back. His right hand slides up her stomach and her ribs, cupping her left breast, squeezing, pinching her nipple, and squeezes again. He leans in and up, starts kissing her neck, lipping her earlobe, kisses her neck, then her lips. Callisto raises herself up off of his lap, but not high enough for him to fall out, then back down. Angellous lifts her up a little and rapidly thrusts himself in and out. Angellous slows to stop, sets her back down in to his lap, and with his left hand, he takes a hold of Callisto's right leg, brings her knee up by his shoulder, and her foot hangs on his side. He reaches down and pulls up her left leg with his right hand to the same position, both knees bent at his shoulders, calf's of her legs pressed up against the outside of his arms. He slides both his hands, one under each ass cheek, supporting her as he lifts her up until just the head remains inside. He drops his arms, forcing her to slam down, violently thrusting back up into her. He continues to brutally violate her in the same position for what seems to be a good half hour. Callisto lowers her legs onto the arms of the chair and raises herself up off Angellous, one leg at a time as she steps down between his legs, off the chair. She kneels down onto the dirt floor between his knees 'n' thighs, proceeds to go down on him, rolling her head while raising up and down for a minute or two. She then slows her head to a stop, slides her lips up off his shaft, up to the bottom edge of the helmet. She's really sucking on him hard. Her cheeks pulled, her breast heaving, she swallows. With her left hand, she takes a hold of his vanilla night stick and pulls him out of her mouth, wiping her chin with her right hand. Still holding on and smiling, she looked up at him. (God damn I wish she would suck my dick. I haven't had a hard on like this in years.) Callisto let go of Angellous' stick, sits back on to her ankles. Angellous stands up, puts himself in his pants, zips up, reaches down taking a hold of Callisto's hand, as she stands as well.

Angellous says to Callisto, "Get dressed. We have a lesson to teach!"

"Callisto walks over to the water barrel. Quickly with the soaked sponge, she washes herself down, walks back over to the chair, and picks up her clothes and gets dressed. Callisto walks back to Angellous, kisses him, and grabs his ass. Angellous walks out of the room. Callisto throws something at me. It's the key. She must have swiped it from his pocket. I picked it up and tried to unlock the waist shackle. Angellous walks back in, slaps Callisto hard across the left side of her face. She spins to the right and falls to the floor. He's coming over. Shit, Shit. It won't unlock.

"He punched me in the back of the head. I wake up on the dirt floor. I must have bounced off the stone wall and fell to the floor. I have a bleeding knot on the right side of my forehead. The back of my head is killing me from where he punched me. Now with a pounding headache, I hear Callisto screaming and crying. I look over. She is completely naked, bent over the side of the rack table. She is face down. Her arms are spread left and right to the top and bottom of the table. It looks like both of her wrist are tied. Her left is tied to the top, her right is tied to the bottom by her wrist, on the rack table. Angellous is standing directly behind her, whipping her back with a six-foot bull whip. Callisto is screaming and crying from the razor cut of the bull- whip, as he snaps into her back again. Her back is all sliced up. He must've whipped her at least thirty times. Angellous finally stops. He walks up against her, pressing his hips up against her ass, as he leans down over the top of her back. She's mumbling; he leans in.

Callisto's crying and trying to say, "I'm sorry. I'm sorry!"

"Angellous leans back up, takes a step back, and unzips and pulls out his trouser monkey with his left hand and puts the head between her ass cheeks.

Callisto begs, "No, please no. I won't do it again, please."

"Angellous thrust hard, up and in. Callisto screams in pain. Angellous continues slamming himself up into her, pulling out, slamming back in, pulling out 'n' slamming back in. He comes. He pulls out. His dick is covered in blood and shit. He reaches up and grabs a hold of the back of Callisto's head by her hair with his left hand. Yanks her head back toward him, lifting her face up off the table. He takes a hold of the whip with his right hand and shows it to her.

Angellous says, "Again; or have you learned?"

Callisto said, "I won't do it again, I promise. I'll do anything you want, anything you tell me to do. I promise!"

"Angellous leans back up, turns, and walks over to the water barrel and washes himself off. He takes his time walking back to Callisto strapped to the rack table. As she lays there crying, he walks to the head of the table, unstraps her left wrist. He walks slowly to the end of the table, squats down, and unstraps her right wrist. As she slowly pulls her arms into her body, he picks up her clothes off the dirt floor, stands back up, and throws them at her.

Angellous said, "Let's go!"

"Callisto rushes to get dressed, but moving slow, very slowly. Her back has to be killing her. She puts her panties on one leg at a time. As she moves, her back bleeds more from the whipping she received. She bends down and pulls up, lifting the waist of her skirt up as she steps in and pulls her skirt up, slowly up to her waist. She reaches to the table, picks up her halter top, tries to shake it out, but only realizes it hurts her back even more. She slides her right arm in, her left arm, and pulls it up over her head as her hair presses into her back. She screams, arching her back up and her chest out. She slowly pulls the top down, down her back, then the front down over her breasts. She must be in pure agony, because I could see her crying. She reaches back up to her neck, grabs a hold of her hair, and pulls her hair out from between her halter top and her cut-up back. The whip marks are bleeding through the back of her shirt. She grabs a table with her right hand for support as she cringes in pain!

Angellous says, "Wow."

"Callisto turns and walks slowly to the opening of the hallway. She's walking slightly hunched over and waddling with each step. He must have really tore her ass apart. She leaves the room and continues walking down the hall. Angellous follows her out holding Lieutenant; Grahams hand.

9
STOOL PIGEON

"A few days or a week goes by, the door opens. Angellous and Callisto came back in. I could hear them coming down the hallway. Angellous is the first to walk in the room. He walks directly to the tool table, begins to rummage through the tools. Angellous picks up a jagged-edge knife, walks over to Graham, with his right hand, he reaches to the inside of Grahams thigh, cuts in and down to the bone, pulls the blade, dragging into the muscle, down and around to the front of his thigh. With his right hand, Angellous grabs a hold of the top of Grahams thigh. He squeezes the thigh muscle, as he continues cutting, cutting from his hip to his knee. Removing his left, top thigh muscle from his leg, Angellous turns Graham to the side. Graham is no longer making any bit of fuss, nor any movement. Graham is now dead from hanging upside down for such a long time, and with no tongue, no hand, no skin. I'm surprised he held on for so long.

"Angellous walks to the rack table, sets down the left thigh muscle, turns, and walks back to Graham. Angellous reaches up once again, with the rigid blade in his left hand, and cuts into the inside thigh, down around the front, into the top right-thigh muscle. He grabs a hold of the thigh with his right hand, squeezes the muscle, and cuts up into the bone from the hip to the knee, re-moving Grahams other top thigh muscle. Angellous walks back to the rack table sets down the jagged edge knife, picks up the other muscle and walks over to the grill. He lays both thigh muscles on the grill, then reaches down and lights it.

"Callisto walks in and over to Angellous by the grill, wraps her arms around his waist, resting her head on his chest. Angellous places his left hand on her ass and stands still for a moment. Angellous lets go of her but, grabs both of her shoulders, and pushes her back away from him. With his left hand, he points to the table. Callisto starts to walk away, over to the rack table.

Angellous said, "Take the bowl from the bottom shelf of the tool table and the knife from off the rack table. Cut that pig's throat! Catch the blood in the bowl. Don't spill it! Tomorrow, we'll have blood pudding."

"Callisto walks to the tool table, picks up the bowl from the bottom shelf, walks over to the rack table, and picks up the smooth edge knife. She looks over and smiles at Angellous, turns, and looks at me with the same sadistic smile, then proceeds to walk over to Graham. Callisto leans down, setting the bowl on the dirt floor beneath his head. With her left hand, she grabs Grahams head by his hair and pulls his head back, exposing his neck. With her right hand, she cuts his throat with the jagged-edge knife from ear to ear. Quickly, she then picks the bowl up, following the running trickle of blood with the bowl, trying not to spill a drop. In fear of what Angellous might do to her next, she's trying to catch every last drop of Grahams blood in the bowl.

"Angellous finishes cooking Grahams two thigh muscles. Cuts them up. With a piece in his hand, he walks over to the holding room, squats down, and unlocks the little door, stands up, hunched over, and steps back, opening the little door. He kicks in the bucket and drops the piece of muscle on the dirt floor, then shuts the little door, squats back down, locks the door, and stands back up, laughing.

Angellous said, "You sick Fuck. You ate Grahams manhood. I never would of eaten that! I'd a starved first."

"Angellous walks back to the grill and throws me a chunk of cooked thigh muscle. As I eat. Angellous pulls out another brown lunch bag. He opens it, pulling out more pictures. Starts pinning them up on the cork-board. It looks like all different people. They are all posed. Some tied up, some just posed in a position.

Angellous said, "You do good work, Campbell. I told you once, I'll tell you again, I'm impressed!"

"Sargent; Campbell, so busy trying to eat he never heard a word Angellous said. He's gotta be starving. It's been at least two weeks, with only Grahams manhood to eat. Callisto walks back to the rack table and sets down the bowl of Grahams blood on the top of the rack table.

Angellous said, "Take it to the house and put it in the fridge!" "Callisto quietly picks up the bowl and walks out of the room, down the hallway. Angellous walks to the column and unlatches the chain that Graham is hanging from. He releases the chain, dropping, Lieutenant; William Grahams lifeless body onto the dirt floor. He walks over by Grahams feet, bends down, and takes a hold of the hanger with his right hand and pulls the chain hook of the hanger off. Then he pulls the hanger hook out of Grahams left ankle, then takes a hold of the hanger with his left hand and pulls Grahams right ankle off the hanger hook, then carries the hanger over to the tool table and drops it on top of all the other tools.

Angellous looks around, asked me, "Be my best man?"

I replied, "Best man?"

"Callisto walks back in the room, comes over by me. Angellous grabs a hold of her left hand, pulls it up, and shows me the rock. As She says, "one-and-a-half karat diamond." Angellous said, "She said, yes."

I said to Callisto, "You gonna marry him?"

Callisto, looking at Angellous, says, "I hope so!"

Angellous said, "Get me the green rope!"

"Callisto walks out of the room and down the hall. Angellous walks away, over to the tool table. He picks up two carabiner's, walks over to the column, and pulls the chain, lifting the hook back up off the dirt floor up into the air, about four foot off the floor. Callisto walks back in with the green rope and hands it to Angellous. He unravels the rope, turns Callisto around to face her back. He lifts her right arm up and out to her side, wraps the end of the rope three times around, just above Callisto's right elbow. Then he lowers her arm back down to her side. He then lifted her left arm backwards towards him, while pulling the rope. Both of her elbows are being pulled to the center of her back. He wrapped the rope three times just above her bent left elbow, then pulled tightly again. Then he reaches up with the rope and pulls the rope through the chain hook and back down. He lifts her left leg up and out to her side and wraps the rope around, just above her left knee. With a clove-hitch knot, he tugs tight, then runs the rope down and wraps it around her torso. He ties off with another clove-hitch knot to her waist. He runs the rope back to her left ankle and ties off. She must really be hurting, that rope tugging and dragging against the skin. She keeps making little "ow" sounds. He pulls the rope that is tied to her left ankle toward her back, bending her leg. He wraps the rope around her throat, swoops the rope back under and up to the chain hook, then ties it off.

"Callisto is just standing on one foot. Her bound elbows

and knee are supporting her weight, and her bound ankle is tied to her throat, causing her to gasp for air. If she moves her head down, or tries to extend her left leg, she will choke herself even more. "Angellous walks to the front of her, by her head. He unzips, unbuckles, and drops his pants. He's standing there staring at her, jerking himself off. He comes on her face, in her eyes, a little in her mouth. His cum is dripping off her face onto the floor. Angellous steps out of his pants, then walks around behind Callisto, giving me the moon.

"He lifts her skirt over her waist, lifts her left leg a little bit up with his left arm, and with his right hand, he pulled her panties to the side. Then he grabs his ding a ling. Slapping the lips of her pussy, he separates her lips wide with his head and slides up, between her lips, until her lips covered his helmet. He lets go of his Wang, grabs the right side of her hip with his right hand. Still holding her left leg with his left arm, he pulls her back into himself, choking her while forcing his junk inside her. He lowers her left leg as he pushes her away, allowing her to breath a little more, then lifts her leg and yanks her back against him. Angellous reaches over to the chain coming down the column, takes a hold of the chain, and tugs down, click, click, click, click.

"Lifting Callisto up off the dirt floor as she screams in agony, he yanks her into him and releases her leg as he pushes her away, pulls her leg up as he yanks her back yet again. Callisto's coming. She squirts a little on Angellous' left leg. Some on the floor and a little dripping down her right leg. He continues swinging her away from him, pulling his spitting stick out, then yanking her back, slamming himself up inside her. This goes on several more times. He comes and pulls out. He lets go of her, letting her swing freely. He walks around to the front of her, steps back into his pant legs, and pulls them up, buttons and zips, then walks out of the room and down the hallway, leaving Callisto swinging.

Callisto struggles to say, “You gonna untie me?”

“Angellous keeps walking down the hall. An hour goes by. He’s coming back. He walks up to Callisto, drops his pants, reaches down with his left hand, and pulls her right leg forward and up, forcing the front of her body to turn up, choking her. He puts himself in her and pulls her on and off himself. Callisto is fading in and out as she is suffocating. He thrust harder and harder and harder. He finally comes. He waits until he finishes coming, then pulls out. He steps back and lets her right leg down, flipping her back over to face the ground, allowing her to breathe again. As she swings he turns her to face him.

“He slaps her in the face to wake her up. As she came around, he stuck his meat rod in her mouth. He takes a hold of her head with his left hand, gripping her left breast with his right hand. He swings her out and away, then back to him, ramming his hard-on in her mouth and down her throat. I can tell by the look on his face he is about to come again. He pulls out, spins her around, now holding her hips. He rammed himself up into her. He pulls harder, pushing himself all the way in. She moans as he cums, holding himself fully inside her. He pulls out, leans down, and pulls up his pants, buttons them up, then walks over to the chair, sits down, and falls asleep.

“Couple hours go by, and he wakes up. He walks back over to Callisto, still hanging, and unties the rope from around her neck. Then he unties her ankle and unties her knee, lowering her leg down. She screams. She’s hanging only by her elbows. He reaches over, unhooks and raises the chain, lowering her until her feet are firmly on the ground. She’s now trying to stand on her own. Angellous unhooks the rope from the chain hook, lowering her elbows. Then slowly, he unties her elbows. I notice she’s not dripping. I thought his cum would have ran out of her.

"Now standing upright, he came three times in her and left her hanging, but nothing is dripping. Callisto starts to try walking, or should I say waddling over to the chair. She is dripping now, it's running down both of her legs, dripping to the dirt floor as she walks. Callisto finally makes it to the chair and sits down and falls asleep.

Angellous said to me, "I will see you tomorrow!" As he walked out.

"I hear the door close, and Callisto was out cold. A few hours go by. Callisto finally wakes up. She walks over to me and asked if I needed anything. Then throws up.

I answer, "Yeah, tie my shoelace."

"As she kneels down on her right knee to tie my shoelace, I unzip my pants and pull out my throbbing hard-on. Callisto looks up and tries to pull away. I grab her by her hair, pulled her head back and into me, causing her to say "ow," opening her mouth. I force myself in her mouth. She is trying to fight, trying to pull away, to pull my stiff pecker out of her mouth, but I pulled her in closer, shoving my joy stick down in her throat. As I let her up, she tried to bite, so I pull her head in again, forcing my stiffy deep down in her throat. I cum! (Ahh, man her mouth felt good!) Pulled my shlong out of her mouth, still holding her hair. She spits out my cum, spits at me. I pulled her up by her hair and slammed her face-first into the stone wall. Holding her against the wall, I lift her skirt and pulled her panties to the side.

I say to her, "You should've let me go!"

"Holding her hair with my left hand, my forearm up against her back between her shoulders, I force my sausage between her ass cheeks, and up in. She's fighting, trying to get away, trying to push herself off the wall. I pull her hips in towards me with my right hand. Still holding her by her hair, against a stone wall, I push down into the small of her back with my left elbow. I thrust in and pull out, in and out. I continued for about twenty minutes, until I finally came. I don't know if it's blood, her come, or my come dripping off my balls. But it's warm and feels good. I pulled out and let go of her. She falls to the ground. I wipe off my dick with my left hand. I wipe the blood, cum, and shit off of my hand on her right thigh.

I told her, "Get cleaned up, whore! Before he sees you."

Callisto says to me, "Gonna kill you!"

"Really, you're engaged to him! You cheated on him! Go-head, tell him."

"I'm pregnant, you asshole!"

"Asshole. Yes, your ass was great. Thanks!"

"Callisto gets up and tries to walk over to the water barrel. Drops her skirt and slides her panties down to her ankles. She's dripping. She dips the sponge into the water barrel, saturating the sponge, pulls it up and out of the barrel, and begins washing herself. Scrubbing and scrubbing, her face, her chest, her thighs, the outside of her thighs, the inside of her thighs. She dips the sponge back in the water barrel, pulls it back out, and tries shoving the sponge inside her, to clean herself out. After an hour or so of scrubbing, she gets dressed and walks to the tool table. She grabs an iron rod and walks over to me. She starts beating me with the iron rod. I was laughing hysterically. She gets emotion- al, starts crying, and throws the rod across the room and falls to the floor. Angellous must have walked in, because I never heard the rod hit the floor. He walks to the tool table and drops it, making a racket. He must have caught the iron rod in midair. Callisto spins her head around, gets up, walks over to Angellous.

Angellous said, "What?"

Callisto interrupts, "Sorry, I didn't see you there!"

"Gavin, you all right?"

I answered, "Ya, I'm good!"

Callisto said, "I was bored."

Angellous laughed, then said, "It is our anniversary. We are going out!"

"He grabs a hold of her left hand with his right and pulls her to him. With his left hand holding the small of her back, and his right hand still holding her left hand, he kisses her deeply. They finish kissing and put out the torches, all but one. They walk out of the room, down the hall. The door closes. It's really dark in here, I can barely see Lieutenant; Grahams lifeless body laying on the dirt floor.

I yell over to Campbell and ask, "You okay?"

"Sargent; Campbell replies, "Don't talk to me!"

"I just want out!"

"You've repeatedly raped that girl!"

"Technically yes, however, she was taken. Just like us. I tried a couple times to get us free and was punished each time, worse than the last! She only tried once! She is now his. I only gave her a taste of what she deserves."

"Taken? What she deserves? She's a victim!"

"Well, you heard them. Angellous said, and I quote, 'we are engaged,' and Callisto just said she's pregnant. A victim? No, she's willing. If she was a victim, she would still be in our shoes. Can't be both!"

"That may be true, but you going to jail right along with her!"

"Jail? Man, if we're lucky I won't live through this, and neither will you. They are going to do to us what they did to your partner, Graham!"

"I'm a Police Officer!"

"I don't think they care. Quiet, I hear something!"

"It's been several weeks, we really don't speak to each-other, not much to talk about. The door is opening, hallway is getting brighter. Callisto walks in with the torch. While she is walking around lighting the torches around the room, Angellous walks in. He walks up to the tool table, drops a bag on top of the tool table. Then he walked over to the cork-board, reached in his right back pocket, and pulls out a few pictures. He squats down and starts to pin them up on the cork-board.

Angellous laughs and says, “I am so proud of you Campbell. Two more double homicides!”

Callisto said, “I never knew just how fulfilling it would be!”

Angellous said, “I’m glad you enjoyed. Next time you are on your own!”

“Angellous puts up the last picture. He stands up, turns, and walks back over to the tool table. He opens the bag that he sat down before and pulls out Chinese food. Hands Callisto a pint box and a bottle of water, then points to me. Callisto walks over and drops both the box of food and a bottle of water with a plastic fork on the floor in front of me. I open the pint box. It is beef and broccoli. I start to eat. Angellous pulls out another box and a bottle of water. He reached up to the shelf above the tool table, pulls down a jar, and opens it. He opens the pint box of Chinese food, dips his fingers in the jar, then sprinkles a brown powder over the food. As Callisto walks back to Angellous, he picks up the fork and begins mixing the food up in the container.

“Angellous picks up the bottle water and the one pint contain- er of food and walks over to the holding-room door. He squats down, sets the food and water on the dirt floor, and unlocks the little door. He opened it and slid the pint box of Chinese food and a bottle of water into the room. Quickly, he shuts the little door and locks it.

Campbell said, “Thanks!”

“Angellous stands back up and walks a few feet back over to the cork-board, with this sadistic smile on his face, while staring at the pictures.

Angellous says, "Nine families. nineteen People, not including Marriessa, Graham. Yeah, I think one more, one more will do you nicely."

"Angellous walks over to Grahams lifeless body, leans down, and grabs his right wrist, and drags the body out of the room, down the hall. A few minutes go by, a couple of thuds and bangs. Angellous comes walking back down the hallway into the room. He tosses Callisto the key to Campbell's holding-room door. Callisto walked over to Campbell's door and unlocks the main door and opens it. She reaches inside, grabs a hold of Campbell's hair, and drags him out of the holding room. She dragged him to Angellous, taking a rag out from his front pocket. Angellous squats down and shoves it in Campbell's mouth, then around to the back of his head, like a gag. He ties Campbell's hands together, behind his back, and ties his ankles together.

"Callisto throws the keys on the dirt floor, just outside of my reach. Angellous takes a hold of Campbell's bound ankles and drags Campbell out of the room and down the hallway. I can hear Campbell struggling.

Callisto shouts, "Wait."

I yell to Callisto, "Hey, the keys. I can't reach them. Come on!"

"Callisto just laughed and ran out the room, down the hallway. Slam. The door shut. I'm alone. I take off my pants. By the cuff of the pant leg, I swoop the waist out over the keys. Thirty or forty times, who knows, maybe fifty times. Finally my pants had knocked the keys close enough for me to reach. I stretched out my left leg, trying to grab the keys with my toes. I got them. I pulled the keys closer to me. I reach down pick up the keys, stood back up, and unlocked the shackle that is anchored to the wall and pulled the fucking waist shackle out from around me. I reach down and picked up my pants and ran over to the barbecue, hoping, searching for something, anything to eat.

"Nothing. There is nothing to eat. I ran over to the tool table, knocking tools off onto the floor. I grab the barbed wire wrapped double chain. (shredder) I walked out of the room. Nervously and slowly, I walk down the hallway. Stairs. I see the stone stairs. I start walking up. I don't hear anything. It's dead quiet. I lift up the floor door, just a crack. I peek out. It's dark, really dark. I lift the door up a little more. I don't see anything. I lifted it up 'n' open, I don't see anyone. Although I can't see much, there is light shining through the seams of the closed barn door. Slowly I walk over to the door and pushed the barn door to the side, open- ing it. Wow, that's fucking blinding.

"I run down the path back to the house. I see my truck. (nice) I run over. Quietly, I open the door. I climb in. My keys. Where's my keys? There they are, in the ashtray. I start the truck. Callisto, shit. She sees me. She's opening the side door, she's yelling something. I throw it in reverse and slam down on the gas. She is coming out, out into the driveway. I spin the wheel, hit the brake, and throw it into drive, spin the wheel back and floor it. I look in the rear-view mirror. Callisto is standing in a cloud of dust, waving her hands above her head, as if she was trying to flag me down. I just hauled ass!

***

Back at the Bar, Kasey Jones Pub & Grub

Small-town cops asks, "Before we go, what happens to the cop, Campbell?"

"Well, he went to jail for the Murders!"

"Jail?"

"You gonna let me tell it or what?" I said. Then I went on to say, "Yes, jail! Now I imagine they'd put him in protective custody, him being a cop and all. But on the other hand, he may very well be the block bitch!"

"Nah, Fuck you man! Block bitch, No Fucking way!"

I laughed, "Well, maybe not, or maybe he got himself killed." The small town group of cops say, "Thanks for the amusing story. Go fuck yourself." Excused themselves as they stumbled drunk, mumbling all the way out the door.

"I heard two squad cars start and back out over the gravel parking lot. Everything is quiet except for the footsteps of Alex as he comes out from behind the bar and walks over to the table where the cops were sitting. Alex is carrying a busboy bin and a towel. As he starts loading the glasses into the bin, I can hear the squad cars pull out onto the road, onto Cotton Row (route 616).

"Well, Alex, a few hours of shut eye, then I got to motor!"

"Alright Gavin. May the Devil be left behind you. The tar under your feet and the light from the Gods shine upon your journey!"

"Thanks, Alex."

Gavin has gone. My bar is all but a mess away from being empty. Wow it's four am. Thursday morning. I got cleaned up and went to go home. That Gavin man, he's a twisted cat. I walk out, lock the door behind me. As I turn to walk to my gray shitty pickup truck, I see flashes of light.

***

What is that? As I walk to the other end of the parking lot, I notice it's cop lights. I gotta see this! As I walk down the road,

Cotton Row, away from my bar, getting closer, cop's flashing lights are getting brighter. It is the five, loudmouth small-town cops that were at my bar earlier tonight.

"Hey, what's going on?" I ask

"The one cop responds, "We almost ran her over!"

"Her?"

"She's over there, on the edge of the road!"

I walk past the other cops, over to the EMT's. There is a young, petite girl. She's laying in the dirt, on the edge of the road. She's wrapped in clear plastic. There is not one piece of clothing on her, only the clear plastic she's wrapped in. She has long, black, curly hair that is slightly moving with the soft, crisp breeze of the morning's break. As I get closer, I could see her face. Closer still, standing above her. Bright Green Eyes, such a brilliant look. Captivating. I can not look away. What a breath- taking sight, I, I'm, just amazed.

"Help. Uh o oo, help!" The plastic-wrapped girl struggled to say.

Holy Shit. She's alive. I turn and yell to the small-town cops, "She's alive. She's Alive!"

I turned back and look down at the girl. The EMT's damn near knocked me over as they brushed up into my right arm, shoving me to the side as they squat down to check and look over the girl. The one EMT stood back up and ran over to the bus. I watch him as he opened the rear doors and pulled out the gurney. He quickly rushed back to the girl, pulled the backboard off the gurney, and laid it down in the dirt, alongside her body. The three EMT's rolled her on her side as they slid the backboard in and under her body. They rolled her back down on to her back, onto the backboard. The EMT's grab a hold of the handles of the backboard, lifting the backboard and her up onto the gurney. Two of the EMT's walked the gurney back to and up into the bus. The third EMT ran to the front of the bus, climbed in the driver's seat, and started up the ambulance. As the EMT started the bus, one of the EMT's steps to the back of the bus and closes the doors behind them. I see the bus shake as the driver put it in gear. Sirens are Wailing, lights are flashing, tires are spinning. She's hospital bound.

***

It's now Monday night, not a spit, smoke, stale beer, or a drop of blood on the floor my bar. Our fair Sheriff of Toulon comes walking in.

Sheriff says. "Alex, you got something to tell me!"

I replied. "No, no. Slow tonight. Thinking about closing early."

"Not tonight, you half-wit. Thursday night."

"Thursday. Yeah, Sheriff, Gavin, he could really tell a story, who wee!"

"Alex, I'm gonna need you to come, come with me 'n' explain this mess."

"Well, Sheriff. Not much to explain. This drifter strolls in, just after dark, orders himself a beer and a room. Then he sat down at that there table and started telling this story."

"Story? About what, Alex?"

"Some foe, murdering people 'n' how he was tortured by this guy!"

"He mention a young girl?"

"Yeah. Two, I think. Oh, and get this. Lieutenant; Graham and Sargent; Campbell too!"

"Get a look at this guy, enough to describe him?"

"I'll try, Sheriff. I'll try."

"You going to tell me what I want to know."

"You telling me that girl on the side of the road, beaten

black and blue, bloody, 'n' naked, wrapped in plastic on Thursday night, is one of them there girls I mentioned before?"

"We are hoping she'll tell us."

"That girl is still alive?"

"Fear so. Death may have been better for her!"

***

We get to the sheriff's office and go in.

Sheriff told me, "Stay here. Describe this guy you seen to Charlie here."

"As he walked off into the back, I started describing the drifter.

Sheriff walks back in 'n' says, "You best be fixing to stay the night."

***

Next day at the Hospital

'Deputy Johnny Ray is sitting bedside with the girl.

Sheriff arrives in the room and asks the Deputy, "How's the girl?"

The doc walks in and says, "Let's speak out here. Let the girl rest. She's been brutally and repeatedly raped, beaten, and tortured, and she has given birth."

Sheriff asked, "When will I be able to speak with her? Is she able?"

"Tomorrow, we'll be fine. We'll give a call when she comes around!"

"When can she be moved?"

"If She wakes up, a day or two."

Sheriff asked, "She say anything, Johnny Ray?"

Johnny Ray said, "Just her name, Callisto."

Sheriff says, "Well, get a cup of joe in ya. Is gonna be a long night. Keep me apprised."

***

Back at the Police Station

As I'm given touch ups to my description and story to Deputy Charlie, the phone rings.

Charlie answers the phone, "Hello, hello." Charlie yells to the sheriff, "It's the doc, the doc. Pick up the phone. It's the doc." I can hear the sheriff asking if the girl is alright. "What, she's awake? Is she stable? Can she talk?" Quiet for a moment, then he said, "I'm going to have Johnny Ray bring her in, answer some questions."

Little while later at the sheriff's station, Deputy Johnny Ray comes walking in with the girl who claims her name is Callisto. He walked her past me into a holding-room, sat her down at the desk. She is to the right of me. I can see her through the glass. She is sitting there with her head hung down. I can't believe she's still alive, can't believe how seriously hot she is! The deputy opens the door. As he steps out of the room,

I hear, "Who are you? What happened to you?" The Sheriff asked!

10
INTERROGATION

The girl replied, "Callisto! My name is Callisto. I am his Wife and a Mother!"

Sheriff asked, "Mother, Wife? What do you call your son? Whereabouts your son? What's the guy's name, the father's name? Answer Me!"

"His father, my husband. You know him as the Drifter. His name is Gavin Miguel."

Deputy says, "Gavin Miguel. That's the guy at the bar!"

Sheriff says, "You stay here with the girl and me! Y'all go find that fucker!" As they head out, hoping he is still at the bar hotel, Sheriff turns back to Callisto, asked, "What did this guy do to you?"

Callisto responds, "About ten years ago,

***

"I was walking home from my friend's house, a piece of shit red pickup pulled over about a block up the road from me. Lights were turned off. I could hear it chug as I walked closer. The streetlight blew out. There was no longer any light on the road. I did not hear the truck anymore. 'Hello, hello.'

I jokingly yelled down the road. I heard something. It sounded like a truck door. Still no lights, 'Hello,' I yelled. 'Hello.' Yet no answer. It's quiet. Not even a cricket or bullfrog making any noise. Just eerily quiet. No Life. Nervously, I continued walking. I heard a voice, 'MMMmm, don't you look perty!'

"I screamed, ran into the woods. I ducked behind a tree and crawled under a briar bush. I didn't hear anything. Quiet again. Oh, NO, he grabbed me, he's pulling me out from under the briar bush. I kicked, smacked, yelled, screamed, cursed. All I heard is him laugh! I was swinging and kicking, but he just kept dragging me by my right ankle, down and through the woods. Dragging me over dead, fallen trees, branches, and rotten, dry leaves, on out of the woods. He dragged me out into the road. He kneeled down with his left knee, pressing into my stomach. He opened his left hand and slid his fingers around the sides of my neck, choking me to keep still. I struggled, watching him pull rope from his back pocket with his right hand. He let go my throat. Between choking and trying to breathe with him kneeling on my stomach, I couldn't get anything out. He took a hold of my legs, bending my knees up towards him. He reaches for my ankles and started to tie my ankles together. I tried to kick, but he was on top of me. After he finished tying my ankles together, he pulled his left knee off my stomach and he knelled on the road, rolled me over, in toward him, face down in the road. He grabbed a hold and pulls my arms up behind me. Tightly, he tied my wrists together. Then he lifted my waist and wrapped the rope around a couple of times. Sets me back down on the road and begins to tie my now bound wrist to my bound waist. He stood back up and walked over to the truck, as I lie struggling to get free on the damp road.

"I heard a clunk and a slam. The tailgate. I think he opened the tailgate. I can't see anything. It's pitch black. I can hear his boots clunking on the road, louder and louder as he walks back to me. I tried to roll over onto my side. I can see him. He grabbed the rope bound around my ankles, lifted my knees and thighs up off the road, started dragging me to the truck. The shirt covering my breast became soaked and tearing up. I felt the pavement and road gravel digging, cutting into my breast. As he slowly dragged me to the back of the truck, he let go of the rope binding my ankles, and my legs fell to the road. He bent down over me, slid his left arm between my back and my arms by my elbows, his right arm under my thighs above my knees, and lifted me up. Step forward towards the back to the truck and placed me on the down tailgate of his truck. He rolled me over onto my left side, and with his left hand on my ass and his right on my right shin, he pushed me into the bed of the truck. He just stood there staring at me for a minute, then reached down, pulling up the tailgate of the truck, and slammed it shut.

"I can hear him walk around the back, to the side and up to the front of the truck. I hear the door open. The truck shakes and leans as he climbed in. A moment goes by, and the truck starts. Slowly we start moving. A half-hour, it seemed to be, and we stopped. I can smell the gas. There are people talking. I felt around frantically, searching with my fingers for anything to make noise with. I can't find anything. The truck floor is clean. The voices stopped, truck door is opening again. The truck shake and leans, door slams shut. The truck starts; the truck buckled, then started going. He drove for another hour or hour and a half. Finally we stopped again. The tailgate dropped open.

***

"The guy leaned on the tailgate and reached in, picked up the end of the rope. Slowly he pulled the rope towards himself, pulling me out of the bed of the truck, closer and closer towards him. I was wiggling but I could not get away. The guy picked me up, turned, and carried me away from the truck into what looked like a barn. Once inside, he leaned down and opened a door in the floor. He carried me down some steps. The walls look like big brown rocks. The steps appeared to be the same thing. We get to the bottom. There is a hallway made of stone 'n' rock. He carries me down the hall until the hallway opens up into a room. (It look like a torture dungeon that you would see in the movies.)

"He carried me over to this little door in the wall, set me down on the floor. He turned and opened the door, then dragged me by my feet into the room, dropped my legs, and walked out shutting, locking the door behind him. I'm lying on the dirt floor, there is just a little light shining through the vent of the door. I'm looking around. I can see. There's nothing. I am starving and thirsty. The light coming through the vent has not changed. I cannot tell if it's day or night. Sick from hunger. My stomach was killing me, and I was dry heaving. It seemed like I had been in there for about a week. I hear something. It is him, he's coming back.

"The light through the vent is getting brighter. I hear the lock on the door, unlocking. The door is opening. I'm trying to move away, but with my wrist tied behind my back to my waist and my ankles bound together, I can barely move. He knelled down in the doorway, lighting the little room with the torch. He sets a bottle of water down and a couple pieces of bread on a plate. He sat down on the dirt floor. He leaned the torch against the wall, crawled into the room, slowly and staring as he crawled up to me. He untied my wrist from my waist, and I shimmied my body to the wall. He slid his hands from the middle of my thighs down past my knees, down my shins to my ankles, and untied them. Quickly pulled my knees up to my chest, pulling my feet away from him. He backed himself up out of the room, taking the torch with him. He closed and locked the door again. I rushed across the dirt floor to the bottle of water. I opened it and drank. Choking, gagging as I try to swallow. Grab a piece of bread and I wolf it down. It seemed like days, maybe a week has gone by. The light coming through the vent is getting brighter again. I hear slamming, rummaging around.

"I can hear him mumbling. But I cannot understand what he's saying. The door is unlocking. I yelled, 'Help, somebody help me.'All I heard was laughing as the door continued to open. The big room is really lit up. I am having a hard time seeing. I hear something, It's the guy, 'MMMmm, don't you look perty!' "I screamed, realizing this was the guy that broke into my house just a few weeks ago. He Molested me, Cut me, violated me with his thick fingers, then vigorously and violently fucked the hell out of me, stealing my virginity.

"He stood back up and turned away from me, disappearing into the big room. A few minutes go by, and I begin edging my- self towards the little door. He must have been standing behind the door, because as I peeked my head out of the doorway of the little room, he grabbed me by my hair and dragged me out of the room, across the dirt floor.

"He squatted down, bearing over top of me. He rolled me back over onto my stomach, face down in the dirt, then knelled down on the floor and retied my wrist. He got up and turned around and straddled me, sat on my ass. He pulled my feet up towards him, retied my ankles together. He got up and walked back towards the hallway.

"He left me lying on the dirt floor, for what seemed to be hours. I could hear him singing as he was coming back down the hallway.

"'I like your pants around your feet. I like the dirt that's on your knees. I like the way you look up 'n' say please. You're like my favorite damn disease.'

"He walked like he was strolling in central park on a Sunday. He reached down, grabbed a hold of my arm, and pulled me up onto my feet. The guy forced me to hop across the room to this column where he grabbed a chain that had a hook on it. He latched the hook on the rope around my wrist. He turned and pulled the other end of the chain. Click. Click. Click, pulling my wrists and arms, pulling them up backwards, pulling me up, until I was on my tippy toes. It really hurt. I couldn't stop myself from screaming. I thought my arms would rip out of the socket. I tried to stay still, for fear that my shoulders would break if I tried to move.

"He asked me my name. I answered, 'Callisto. Please let me go. Please. I won't tell anyone. Please.'

"He said, 'They call me, Gavin Miguel.'

"The asshole stepped over to the column and sat down on the dirt floor, staring up at me, just staring. I cursed him out, yelled and screamed. He just sat there, staring up at me with these sole- less eyes and no expression on his face. I started to apologize for bothering him, for cursing at him, for screaming. I swore I would listen. I would do anything. I begged and pleaded. After what seemed like hours, he stood up and walked around, putting out the torches on his way out of the room, leaving me hanging by my wrist, hanging there exhausted, starving, arms and hands numb, shoulders feeling as if being torn out. Left in the dark, I was left all alone. I was alone!

"I think he was gone for a couple of days. He came back in and re-lit the torches, set a bag on a table filled with what looked like tools, turned to me, walked over, and he sat back down in front of the column, staring back up at me. After a little while, he asked if I would like to eat. Eagerly I answered, 'yes.' He stood back up and walked over to this tool table, where the bag he brought in with him was.

"He opened the bag, pulled out a plastic to-go container. He walked back over to me, opened the container, and pulled out a spoon. He knelled down in front of me. I don't know what it is. It smelt awful and it looked like bright red pudding. He dipped the spoon in, lifting out a spoon full of this goop, then slowly he raised it up to my chin. As I open my mouth,

he said, 'behave!'

I answered, 'yes!'

"As he placed the spoon in my mouth, allowing me to have a bite. It tasted really good. He continued to feed me until there was nothing left. When I finished my last bite, he wiped my lips clean. He stood back up, turned, and walked away. He walked back to the tool table.

I asked him, 'What was it that he fed me?'

He replied, 'Blood pudding.'

"I gagged, tried to throw it up, but nothing would come out. He'd just laughed and walked out the room.

"This went on for days, maybe weeks. Every couple of days he would come in 'n' sit for a little while, watching me, then he would ask me if I would like to eat, then he would feed me more that disgusting-smelling, great tasting blood pudding. Few times he would give me raw, bloody meat. Every time he would laugh on his way out, until the one day came that I did not gag, I did not heave.

"At the tool table, he stood waiting for me to gag. Realizing I was not going to,

he turned and asked me, 'What is it you need?'

I raised my head, looked up at him and said, 'I need to go to the bathroom.'

"He walked over to me, knelled down and untied my

ankles, stood back up and walked to the column, unhooked the chain, raising it up, lowering my wrist back down to my waist. I stood straight up for the first time in over a month. Slowly he unhooked the chain from my wrist, turned me around by my shoulders, facing me towards the far back wall. He reaches on out in front of me, pointing to a bucket against the wall. As we started walking over,

I asked, 'are you going to untie my hands?'

"He didn't say a word. We get to the bucket against the wall. He reached down and slid the bucket in toward us. He turned me around to face him, lifted my head by my chin, and stared in my face. He slowly lowered his hand down my neck over my collarbone, down over the top of my left breast, cupping under- neath and pushing back up, squeezing my tit. After a second he released my breast, and both his hands met together at the front button of my mini-skirt. Staring at him, I start to cry, tears rolling down my cheeks and down off my chin.

"He unbuttons my skirt and unzips the three inch zipper. He slid his thumbs between the skirt and my skin, slid his hands to the sides of my body. He began lowering my skirt and my red laced thong panties down to my knees. He stepped to the side of me. He slid his right arm between my arms and my back, then he slid his left arm in front of me, under my breast, grabbing a hold, tightly grabbing my right tit, as he said, 'Sit back. I have you!'

"Trying to save some humility, I sat back as he lowered me down to the top edge of the bucket. I began to pee. Before I was finished, I started to defecate. Scared shitless, I apologized to him. After I finished, I leaned up and forward. Still holding my right breast with his left hand, he pulled out his right arm from between my arms and my back. He reached down to the floor, pulling a couple tissues out of a box that was next to the bucket. He reached up between my legs with a tissue and began wiping me. Slowly and gently, he wiped me clean.

"He let go of me as I stood up straight. He stepped to the front of me and pulled up my red lace thong panties, then reached back down and pulled up my miniskirt and re-buttoned it. He placed his right hand on my back and said, 'table,' then shoved me. I walked to the table. He spun me around to face him and grab a hold of my waist. He lifted me up to sit on the table. He reached down and grab a hold of my ankles and lifted my feet up on the table, spinning me sideways.

"He pulled my feet towards the end of the table and pulled up straps from the corners, bound my ankles to the end of the table with what felt like leather straps. He walked back up towards me, reach behind my back with a knife that he pulled from a sheath hanging from his belt, and cut my wrist free. He put his right hand on my right shoulder and gently push me back to lie down. He raised my right arm up over my head to the top the table and tied my right hand down. He walked to the other side of the table, raise my left arm, and tied my left hand down to the other corner of the table. He began sliding his fingers gently down the inside of my arm. He leaned over me and kissed my belly. Then he stood back up, turned, and walked out of the room, leaving me tied down, unable to get away.

"A day later, he comes back in with a bottle of water. He walked to the side of me and slid his left hand under my head, lifted my head up, allowing me to drink some water. After a few swallows, he walked away and set the bottled water down on the tool table. He pulled out this machine from underneath the table. He dragged the machine over to the top end of the table, unwound these thick wire cables from the handle. He walked around the table and opened up this little door in the wall. He reached in, dipped something into a barrel, took a step back, stood up, and turned around facing me. It was sponges. He had sponges in his hand and they were dripping wet.

"He walk back around to the other side of the table, by the machine. On the end of the thick wire cables were clamps. He squeezed the clamp handles one-by-one placing each sponge in- side each of the clamps. He lifted my left knee and placed the one sponge underneath my right calf. Then he reached down and turn the machine on. He waved the other sponge above my body. As I begged and pleaded him not to touch me with that, he grazed my right arm, electrocuting me. My body lunged, my jaw clenched shut. He pulled the sponge away from me. He begins grazing my inner thigh with his right hand. Slowly he worked his hand up to the lips of my pussy,

I yell out, 'NO!'

"He grabbed a hold of my panties, yanked them to the side.

I said, 'Please, please no.'

"With this sadistic smile, he jammed his thick fingers up in- side of me. He continued, shoving his fingers up inside, out and back up inside, deeper and deeper each time. He continued fingering me for a few minutes. I came, like I've never came before. He pulled his fingers out and licked them clean, still with that smile on his face. He reaches over my mid-drift with the sponge in his left hand and placed it on my left hip, holding it there electrocuting me for only a moment, but for what seemed like several minutes. He pulled the sponge off only after I came. He took a step back from the table, pulled the other sponge out from under my calf. He dropped both cables onto the dirt floor and shut the machine off.

"He unbuttons and dropped his pants to his ankles, climbed up onto the table, up on top of me. With his knees on each side of my body and his balls lying on my stomach, he pulls my shirt up and over, bearing my breast. He leans up, kneeling, takes a hold of the outside of my tits, pressing them together, wrapping them around his thick, long stick. He began moving my breast up towards my chin, back towards my stomach, jerking himself off. I could feel it throbbing. A couple minutes go by and he starts to come. He came on my jaw, my neck. He climbed off of me, step back down onto the dirt floor.

I said to him, 'I fucking hate you!'

"He turned and walked out of the room.

"About a day went by. I can hear him walking back in.

He walks up to me and asked me, 'behave? obey?'

"Scared out of my mind, starving, and having to go to the bathroom,

I replied, 'Yes, I will behave, I will do what you ask of me!'

"He walks to the end of the table, unstraps both of my legs. He turns and walks back up to the top the table by my hands, unties my right hand and walked to the center of the table. He unbuttons, unzips his pants. He pulled himself out,

He said, 'You can move your hand!'

"Then pulled my hand to him. I didn't know what to do. I did not know what he would do to me if I didn't do what he told me to do, so I began massaging his balls. Once he was erect, I began jerking him off. I could barely get my fingers to meet. It took a while for him to cum.

"For weeks, months, this went on. I would allow him to do things to me. In return he would allow me more freedom. If I missed behave or hesitated, I would be punished. He would electrocute me, cut me, strap me to a device and have his way with me or he would whip me, tie me back up and hang me from the hook while forcing himself in me. He even beat me like a child. I don't know how long it took. I don't know when it was. My only concern and thought became the fulfillment of his desire. I became so good, loyal, and devoted. He allowed me to come back with him to his house. He allowed me to leave the dungeon.

***

I began cooking and washing his clothes. I even cleaned the house daily. Anytime the notion enter his mind, I'd stop what I was doing to satisfy him.

One day he asked, 'If I'd like to go to the store?'

"Excited, I jumped on him, wrapping my legs around his waist, kissing his cheek, kissing his lips, kissing all over his face. For the first time, I initiated it. I climb down off of him, undid his pants, pulled out his pudgy, and placed it in my mouth, wrapping my tongue around the head and sucking. It only took a minute or two, I swallowed. Then I stood up 'n' dropped my pants, turned around, bent over and reached up between my legs, reached up behind me, taking a hold of him, and put his big spitting stick inside of me. He came inside me and continued, until he came a second time,

Then he said, 'Let's go.'

"I rushed to cleaned myself up and to get dressed. Out the door we went. We drove for about an hour.

***

We arrive at this little town butcher shop and general store. We got out of the truck and went inside. We begin shopping, picking up little things here and there. We walk back out with the bags and put them in behind the back seat. Gavin told me there was a coffee shop around the corner, to go and get us Coffee. I leaned over and kissed him, spun around, and hopped out of the truck. I couldn't believe he was trusting me. I can't let him down, so quickly I rushed around the corner to the coffee shop, ordered us each a mocha crap-a-chino, Impatiently waiting. Finally they finished making our coffee. I threw the money on the counter, grabbed the coffees, and ran out the door. I ran down the street, back around the corner to where we parked, but he was gone. The truck was not there. I sat there, on the stoop of the general store, waiting for Gavin to come back.

The owner of the store asked, 'Are you alright. Do you need anything? Is there someone I could call for you?'

I told him, 'no,' that he was coming back for me.

"It's now getting dark. I started walking, trying to walk back to the house, but I'm not really sure where I was going. I was walking for about an hour, hour and a half. Then I heard this loud truck roaring up the road, coming from behind me. I stopped and turned around. It's him, it's Gavin and the shitty redneck pickup. He pulls up and slammed on the brakes in front of me. He jumped out of the truck, ran back to me. He grabbed a hold of me, and I dropped the coffees. He wrestled me to the ground, shoving my face into the dirt road. He retied my wrists together, tied my ankles together, then he bent my legs, pulling my ankles up towards my ass and tied them to my wrist. He picked me up, as he stood up, turned, and walked back to the back of the truck, lifted me up over the tailgate, and dropped me into the bed of the truck. He walk back around the side and climbed back into the truck, put it in gear, and spun the tires as he pulled off. He never said a word. I don't understand what I did wrong. I was rolling around the bed of the truck as he drove like a lunatic.

***

"Only a few minutes went by. I see the side of the house as we pass, driving up into the back field. We come to a stop. Door opened. Gavin walked around the truck and open the barn doors. He came back to the back of the truck, dropped the tailgate, reached in, taking a hold of the rope that he hogtied me with.

I asked him, 'What did I do?'

He looked to his right and said, 'You gonna help? Grab the fucking rope!'

"He lifted me up over his shoulder, carried me into the barn. He leaned down, grabbing the door that is in the floor, lifted it up, opening it. He carries me down the steps, down the hallway. Once in the room, he dropped me onto the dirt floor.

"He walked back across the room, opened up a little door, and pointed.

He said, 'Can you get that?'

"Then he shut the door and locked it. He then walked back to me and squatted down, grabbed a hold of my legs, and cut the rope from around my ankles, stood up and reached down, grabbing a hold of my arms, and stood me up onto my feet. He forced me to walk across the room past the first column, towards the second column. The jerk held my bound wrist with his left hand and was shoving my back with his right. He switched hands and held my bound wrist with his right hand. He reached to the column with his left, grabbing the chain with the hook on it. He unhooks the chain from the column and raises the chain into the air, lowering the hook-end down over me. He wrapped the hook around the rope, binding my wrist. He reached back over with his left hand and tugged on the other end of the chain, raising the hook back up into the air. He pulls down the other end of the chain against the column. Click. Click. Click, lifting my wrists and arms, lifting them up backwards. Much like the first time, that really hurt. I couldn't stop the tears from falling.

"He growled and looked at the little room door, then turned back, stared at me with this look of amazement. He pulled out a knife. I don't know where he got it from. Gavin Miguel slides his left hand up over my collarbone, to my shoulder, scrunching my shirt. With his right hand, he slides the blade of the fillet knife under the collar of the shirt, following his fingers down over my shoulder, down until the blade came out the bottom of my sleeve. I jumped. 'Ow, get off me, you son of a bitch, You cut me.'

"As I watch, Gavin continued cutting my shirt off of my arm and shoulder. As it fell forward, hanging over my breast, he leans in and lick the blood off my arm. He squatted down and turned me sideways, retied my ankles together. As he stood up, he lifted my feet off the dirt floor. As he lifted my feet off the dirt floor, my knees bent, forcing all my body weight on my already, almost dislocated shoulders. He lifted my feet up and latches the hook on the rope binding my ankles.

"Crying at this point, pleading and begging him to stop, 'Please stop Gavin please?'

"He lifted my head by my chin with his right hand. He stared in my face as he softly wiped away the tears from my eyes and off my cheeks, then he leaned in and kissed me ever so gently, almost that of seduction. He walked over to the tool table and grabbed this ball with leather straps and walked back to me. He forced the ball in my mouth, pulling the straps around both sides of my face to the back of my head and latched them together. Gavin walked around the room, putting out the torches, leaving only one torch lit as he walks out of the room and down the hall- way that's made of stone boulders. The same design and structure as the room that I was hanging in before.

"Day or two goes by. I no longer have feeling in my arms, hands, knees, and my feet are so numb from the lack of blood. Even the tingling and needles stopped. Gavin is coming. Shit; Shit, what do I do? Fuck, He's gonna kill me. But all I could do is cry. He walks in the room. He re-lights all of the torches as he walks around the room. Arrogant Son of a Bitch has food. Man, I'm freaking hungry. Sets down the food on the dirt floor. Thank god he's coming over with food. He reached up behind my head, unlatched the mouth gag, and slowly pulled the straps out from around the sides of my head. Gently he pulled the ball out of my mouth. He reaches down to the floor, picked up the box, stood back up, and opened it. It was chicken and broccoli. Gavin sticks a fork in the box and pulls out a piece of broccoli, tries to feed it to me.

"I said, 'What the fuck Gavin. I'm not a child! Fucking Asshole, untie me and I'll feed my self!'

"He kept trying to feed me. I tried to bite his fingers. He slapped my face with his left hand. I tried to bite him again, then he slapped me harder. With his right hand he tried to feed me again, so I took a few mouthfuls. Damn it tasted good. He caressed my cheek and grazed his fingertips down my neck.

"I spit a mouth-full of food in his face and said, 'Fucking touch me!'

"Gavin dropped the food and walked away. He then stopped, turned back around, and walked to the column, unlatched the chain that's holding me up, lowered me down one foot. He reached up behind me and unhooked my ankles from a chain, lowering my legs to the dirt floor. Squatted down in front of me and looked up, holding my ankle as he stared for a moment. Then he untied the rope from my ankles. I tried to kick him. I really wanted to kick him. But I could hardly lift my leg. He turns into me, with his back against me, lifting my leg, he removed my left calf-high buckle boot, set my stocking-covered foot back down onto the dirt floor. He then grabbed and lifted my right leg, pulling me into him to remove my right calf-high buckle boot. Slowly he leaned down, setting my stocking-covered foot on the dirt floor. With the blood racing down my legs to my feet, it hurt, the throbbing, pulsing of the blood rushing through my legs. He stood up, stepping away, turned from me, which actually made him face me. My stocking-covered toes are barely on the dirt floor, just barely relieving my body weight from my almost broken shoulders and tied wrist. As I tearfully filled with pain, he had this dull, lifeless expression on his face and a look in his eyes of a kid in a candy store. I became hysterical, flailing around trying to get loose.

"Gavin sits down on the dirt floor against the column, staring up at me as if he was undressing me with each vibration of his eyes. Each twitch, another piece of clothing was removed. A while goes by. His look became a goofy little smirk. He stood up, walked up against me.

He asked, 'what do you want?'

I answered, 'Let me go, just let me go!'

"What do you need?'

"'I need to pee!'

"With a smile on his face, he inhaled and stepped to the side of me. With his left arm supporting my mid-drift, lifted me up as he unlatch my bound wrist from the chain hook, then set me down, so I was standing on my feet, supporting myself. I quickly tried to step away and fell. He leaned down over top of me, grabbed my arms just below my shoulders, and lifted me back up. Holding my arm with his right hand, he squatted down beside me and started wiping the dirt off of my breast, the front of my thighs of my skirt. He walked me over to the corner of the room to a bucket.

He told me, 'This one is yours. Behave or I will take it away!' "He stood in front of me, unbuttoning and unzipped my skirt

as I cried silently, taking his time pulling my skirt down to my knees. He slid his hands up my outside thighs. I tried to kick him, and he caught my shin.

He said, 'That's one, next your bucket!'

"He slid his hands once again up the outside of my thighs, to my hips, taking a hold of my red-lace panties. Slowly he pulled them down to meet my skirt at my knees. He reached between my legs, grabbing the bucket from behind me and pulling it up behind my legs. He then stood up, stepped aside, and then stepped behind me. He slid his hands, his arms between my ribs and my arms, wrapping around the front of my body, crossing his arms and grabbing a hold of both of my breast. He tugs me back towards him,

He says, 'Sit back. I have you!'

"Nervously I try 'n' pee. I almost can't. I finished peeing. He stands me up, walks around to the front of me. He leans down and grabs a box of tissues, pulls out two. He folds them up, reaches between my thighs, sliding his hands up to my Cooch, and begins to wipe for me as he stares in my face. He finished wiping me and he tosses the tissues in the bucket behind me, squats down on my side, turns me to him, and slowly pulls up my red-lace panties, while deeply inhaling with a smirk on his face. He still left my skirt scrunched down around my knees, spun me around. With his right hand, he pushed my back forward, forcing me to walk. He continued pushing me as I walked, pushing me past the table over to the restraint chair.

"He grabs my arm, stopping me from walking. He stepped to his right and turn me to face him. With my back to the chair, softly he pushed me backward, sitting me down into this, what looks to be a porch chair with straps. He leans down over me, unties my bound wrist, then pulls both my hands to each of the arms of the chair, straps my wrist to the arms of the chair. He squats down in front of me. I'm debating if I should try to kick him again. He grabs my right leg and straps my shin to the leg of the chair. He turns slightly to his right and straps my left shin to the leg of the chair. He stood back up, smiles at me, turns, and walked out the room.

"A few hours go by, and he comes back in with a bag of what smells like Chinese food and a bottle of water. He sets the bag of food down the tool table and pulls out a couple boxes. He opens it up and walks over to me, squats down between my legs, and opens up another box. It is lomein. He put the bottle water between my thighs, sticks a fork in the lomein, and begins to feed me. I'm starving. I choke a little, but it's so good. I can't eat quick enough. He gives me a sip of water and then feeds me the rest of the lomein. After a few minutes of staring at me, he let me drink the rest of the water. He stood up and walks to the tool table, throws the food containers in the bin of garbage at the left end of the tool table. He then walked around the room, putting out the torches on his way out and down the hallway. I just cried myself to sleep.

"I wake up to yelling and screaming, as a young girl is yelling, 'Ugly mother Fucker, unhand me!'

"He dragged her by her bound wrist into the room, past me to the chain hook that I once hung from. Gavin lifted her up and latched the chain hook onto her rope-bound wrist and walks to the column, tugs the chain down, raising her arms above her head and pulling her up until her feet aren't even touching the dirt floor. The new girl's cursing at him, screaming at my Gavin, trying to kick him. After ten minutes of her mouth, he went to the tool table and grabbed this cylinder mouth gag, forced the cylinder into her mouth and tightly buckled the straps behind her head.

"Gavin walks to the back of the room by the small doors and dips a bucket into a barrel and walks back over, holding the bucket. He douses me with the bucket of water. He then walked back around me, back to the barrel, and dipped the bucket again, walked over to the new girl with the bucket and doused her as well. He set the bucket down on the dirt floor by the column. Then he began cutting her. Short and shallow cuts, slowly he cut, hundreds of cuts on her arms, stomach and thighs.

"I told the girl, 'If she doesn't Calm down, it will only get worse!' Then I asked Gavin, 'Am I not enough?'

"Gavin was talking to someone on his right, but there was no one there. He just ignored my comment and took his time cutting away her clothes. He vigorously and violently violated her, stealing her virginity as she screamed this ungodly scream. He beat her a little. Occasionally he stopped and gave her electric shock with the battery charger, but only after he had shocked himself. Then he went back to do a lot more cutting. He takes the knife and shoved it in her right thigh, about half of the blade was in her leg. Marriessa screams. He pulls the blade out of her thigh, lifted her leg as he squatted down onto one knee and drank from her cut. When he finished, he sewed up the cut on her thigh. He dropped her leg back down, stood up,

"He finally lowered the chain, lowering her back down to the ground, down to her knees, and unhook the chain from her bound wrist. He picked her up around her waist and carried her over to the rack table, lifted her up, and dropped her on top of the table. He pulled this bent metal thing out and slid it around her head, placed her arms and ankles in this brace thing, turned, looked at me, smiled, turned back and repeatedly raped this girl while pulling this barbwire wrapped chain over her body. A couple hours go by. He finally stopped.

"He walks back over to me, squats down, and steadily molest my body, grazing his fingertips from the top of my neck, to my ear, slowly down my neck and over my collarbone, down my chest plate between my breast. Up under and cupping my left breast, as if it was his to play with. He continued sliding his hands down to my mid-drift, my waist. over my every curve and tone line. He reached down, unstrapped my left leg. He lifts up my leg by my foot and extended my leg out. I kicked him. He fell back onto his ass. He picked himself up off the dirt floor. "He said, 'Consequences.'

"Grabbed my foot, broke my big toe. I screamed in agony and I promised not to do it again. Then he reset my big toe and walked out of the room.

"A half hour went by. I hear him walking down the hallway, coming back to the room. He comes into the room, and I notice he has a two bags, one of which is full of ice. He walked over to me and iced my big toe. He stood back up, walked over to the tool table with one of the bags, pulled out a couple boxes of food. He set them down on the table, grabbed one box, walked over to me. He squats down, opens the box, and begins to feed me. I took my time eating. It was so good. When I finished, he got up and walked around the room. I heard him talking.

"He was saying, 'Feed your girl but control her!'

"I have no idea who in the hell he is talking to. It was just me and Marriessa. He sets a camera on the shelf above the tool table and starts feeding Marriessa. He finishes feeding her, throws all the containers into the garbage by the tool table. He walk to the other end of the table and pulls out the battery charger and sponges. He soaks the sponges with the left-over water in the bucket by the column, connected the sponges to the cables, and begins to argue with himself.

"He said, 'Here, I'll show you!'

"Then shocked himself. It knocked him on his ass. After min- ute, he got up, picked up the cables, staring up at her, and began shocking her. A few minutes goes by. He stops, drops the cables on the ground 'n' turned, walked over to me and unstrapped me from the chair and allowed me to go to the bathroom on my own. As I finished, he walked over, picked up the tissues, and wiped for me. He walked a couple steps away, to the back wall, grabbed a waist shackle, walked back over to me, strapped it around my waist. The shackle was connected to a chain that was anchored to the wall.

"Gavin smiled at me, turned and walked over to Marriessa, to the rack table, walked to the end of the table and climbed up, lying on his stomach, and began eating her out. After she came, he got up off the table, walked over to me, and unlock the waist shackle.

"'You gonna?'

I interrupted him and said, 'Yes, I'll do anything you want!' "He turned me around to face the wall and rebound my wrist behind my back, then walked me over to the Podium chair, that he called; the Garrett. He lifted my arms over the back board, and sat me down. Reached behind my head, pulling this strap out and around my neck, then to the back of the backboard, pulling it tight, restricting my air. He walk back to the front of me and squatted down. He slid his right hand up under my ass. He lifted me up and started to lick my lips, flicking my clitoris with his tongue. As I slightly suffocated from the neck strap, I came. It was as if I burst. He lowered my ass back down, pulled his hand out from under me, stood up. He steps in, stepped over each of my legs. With his right leg on my left side and his left leg on my right, he unzips his pants, pulled out his meat club, and began to jerk off while staring in my face. A few minutes went by, and he came. He came in my eye, on my face. He steps in towards me, grabs my head by my hair, and shoved the head of his vanilla pole in my mouth. As I roll my tongue around the head, I noticed his life juice is dripping off my cheek onto my breast. I began sucking deeply. He came again, this time in my mouth. I tried to pull away, to spit it out. He grabbed my head and pulled me in closer, shoving more of his penis in my mouth. I had no choice but to swallow.

"When he finished, he walked over to the column, picked up the bucket, walked over to the barrel, and refill it with water. Then, with the full bucket of water, he walked over to Marriessa and doused her with the water again. He turned and walked to the tool table and grabbed a glass jar and walked back to Marriessa. He opens the lid of the glass jar, dipping his fingers inside, pulling out this powder, white powder. With a handful, he drizzles it over her body and laughed as her skin boiled and she screamed. After a few minutes of this horrifying scream, he poured vinegar over her body, drenching her, stopping the skin from burning. He turns and walks back to the tool table and sets the vinegar and jar of powder down on the tool table. Then walks over to me and un- straps my neck from the back post of the podium chair. He walks to the front of me, grabbing my arms, and stands me up, turns me to face away from him, and unbinds my wrist. He turned me back around to face him. With his right hand, he caressed my left cheek as he smiled for the second time. He turned me around as he hands me a towel. We walk side-by-side over to the rack table, to Marriessa. I removed the restraint brace, grab her bound wrist, pulling her arms up over her head up to the top of the table, and strapped her down, binding her wrist to the table. I walked to the end of the table, grabbed her legs one at a time, strapping each leg to the bottom corners of the table.

"Gavin hands me a knife and says, 'Short and shallow!'

"So I begin to cut her. I cut her a lot. He steps behind me, took a hold of my left hand, and placed it on Marriessa's left breast. He squeezed my hand, squeezing her firm breast. Together we lifted her breast up off her body. He took my right hand holding the knife and force my hand to cut the skin from her breast, slowly cutting from the outer left side, down to the bot- tom, up between her breast to the inside of her left breast. Then he places my fingers to grab the skin on the outer left side of her breast, forced my right hand to cut up under. While peeling back the skin, he let go my hands.

“He said, ‘Finish skinning her breast. Follow the muscle and cut her breast completely off. Fillet it from the center to the nipple for lunch!’

“I was so afraid of what he do to me next. I went along with it. I skinned the skin from her tit and then slowly cut away the muscle of her breast, removing her boob from her body. Whole time, she screamed this terrifying, hysterical, bone-tingling scream. Once I finish removing her breast, I set it on the table, cutting from the center down to were the nipple would be, picked up both pieces and walked around the table to this little barbecue. Then layed each piece on the rack of the barbecue.

“Gavin walked over to me with a pair of tongs, pulled out a metal plate from the coals of the grill. The plate was glowing amber as he walked over and placed the plate on Marriessa’s chest where her left breast used to be. Her body launched up into an arch, then collapsed as she passed out. I can hear the sizzling of her body burning from here. Her boob was done cooking so I pulled it off the grates and layed the meat on a plate, and cut it up. Gavin and I eat a piece or two.

“When we finished eating, Gavin softly took a hold of my hand. We walk out of the room and down the hallway.

***

“We walked out to his truck. He open the door for me. I climb in, then he shut the truck door. As he walked around, I leaned over and open the driver’s door for him. He climbed in, started the truck. He put his hand on my thigh as we pulled off.”

11
THE FRAME

"We pull up to this house in the suburbs, knocked on the door claiming that our truck broke down and seeing if we can use their phone. We went inside, and Gavin forced me to help him torture and murder the family. We walked out the back door, through the yard, and through the neighbor's yard, opened up the sliding doors to the kitchen, walked in. We murdered and slaughtered that family as well. As we were finishing, he heard a noise upstairs. We walk up the stairs and found out they had a couple visiting them. We murdered them and mutilated their bodies. Then he went around carving a mark on the back of each of their necks. When he was finished, we walked out, walk back down to the truck, and pulled off. We drove for a bit.

***

"Gavin said to me, 'Pick out a house and show me what you've learned.'

I pointed and said, 'That one.'

"It was a cute little ranch house, looked almost like a cottage. He stopped, and we walked to the door. Finally, after nine days of instruction, he let me torture and murder my first family all by myself. As he quietly watch. I became overzealous and mutilated the young boy.

***

Back at the sheriffs Office

"You see, I had to prove, prove myself. To prove that I am worthy.

***

"There was this girl, not much older than me, that opened the door. We told her like the first house. Our truck broke down,

We ask, 'Can we use the phone.'

She stepped back from the door and said, 'Come on in.' "We looked at each other and step through the doorway. She closed the door and said, 'The phone is this way.'

"She walked in front of us, heading down the hall. With my left hand, I grabbed her by the hair of the back of her head and pulled back. I grabbed her right wrist and pulled it up, back up behind her back towards her shoulders.

"She screamed, 'Ow. What are you doing?'

I said, 'Shut up bitch!'

"I force her down the hallway into the kitchen, up to the center-island counter. I let go of her arm, but not her hair. I walked around the counter. With both hands on each side of her head, I yanked down on her head by her hair, bouncing her face

walked back into the kitchen. I rummage through the drawers of the kitchen and found this spatula. I laid his junk on the counter, slid a knife from the bottom, up inside to the head, slid the knife back out, set the knife down, and picked up the spatula. Holding the base skin of his father's dick, I slipped the handle of the spatula up inside, the full length of the skin on up to the head. I walk over to the boy, grabbing the kid by the hair of his head, and shoved his face into his mother's wet, cum-dripping pussy.

Told him, 'Start licking.'

"As I held his head and his face buried in to his mother's crotch, I shoved the skin-covered handle of the spatula up inside the boy's ass. As I pulled out the spatula, the skin of his father's penis stayed inside the boy's ass. Only the old man's balls were left hanging out. Gavin just laughed. After his mother came, I drag the boy by his feet from his mother. His chin, cheeks, lips, and nose glisten with the life juices of himself and her.

"I leaned back up, reached up to the counter, pulled two knives from the knife block, and began cutting and slicing the shit out of the boy's mother. The blood, the screaming was intoxicating. She was slowly dying from bleeding out. I stopped cutting. I tied the boy up even more, rolled him on his back, and pushed his knees to the sides of his rib cage, exposing his boyhood and the balls of his father, hanging out of his little ass. I pulled open the oven door, leaned down, and picked him up, shoved him into the oven, and set it to 450°. I propped his mother against the center-island counter in front of the oven to watch her son be cooked to death as she bled out.

"Gavin went from the mother, upstairs, to the father and carved a symbol on the back of his neck. When he finished, we left, only to be pulled over by a redneck Lieutenant and over-zealous Sargent. Not even twenty miles from the family I just slaughtered.

***

"We pulled over to the side of the road, half on the pavement and half on the dirt shoulder. This long-haired snaggle tooth with a nine o'clock shadow walks up to the driver's side, up to Gavin. A clean-cut stickup the ass Sargent, taking his sweet time, walked up my side of the truck. The Lieutenant knocked on Gavin's window as he is rolling it down.

The Lieutenant says, 'License and registration!'

Gavin said, 'Let me find it. It's here somewhere!'

Sargent says to me, 'Ma'am are you all right? I noticed a bit of blood on your Shirt!'

"Gavin smiles at me and opens the driver's door to step out. The Lieutenant points to the back of the truck.

Sargent asked me again, 'He hurt you?'

"I hear a thud. The truck rocked foreword. The Lieutenant shoved Gavin against the tailgate.

Lieutenant says, 'Don't move, if you know what's good for you. Sargent; come here. Run his papers.'

"Sargent walks to the back of the truck to Gavin and the Lieutenant, takes the papers, and walks towards the police cruiser. I get out of the truck, see Gavin spin around, punching the Lieutenant square in the mouth. The Lieutenant falls backwards down on to the dirt side of the road. Gavin jumps on top of the Lieutenant and continues punching him in the face. I reach back into the cab of the truck, grabbed the 357 pistol off of the seat, and run back to the cop car, shoving the tip of the barrel against the side of the Sargent's head.

I said to the cop, 'Step back and get on the ground, now!'

Sargent says, ‘Okay, okay, calm down, now just, just take it easy!’

‘On the ground, PIG!’

“The sergeant lies face down in the dirt with his hands up and out by the top of his shoulders. I leaned down over top of him, pulled his gun out of his holster, placed it on the ground, and handcuffed him with his own handcuffs. I leaned back up and stood there, pointing my gun at him as Gavin rolled the lieutenant over and handcuffed him with his own handcuffs. Then he stood him up and walked him over to me. Gavin let go of him, and he fell down onto the sergeant’s back. Gavin leaned down, slid his left arm around the sergeant stomach, his right hand on the cop’s cuffed wrist, and lifted the sergeant up, walked him to the back of the truck. He brought his arm out from around the sergeant, punched him in the back of his head, knocking out the sergeant. Sargent drops face first into the dirt. Gavin lifted up the sergeant’s legs, resting his feet on the tailgate of the truck, leans down, picks him up by his arms, sliding his feet into the bed and shoving the sergeant into the bed of the truck. He turns around, wiped his chin with his right hand, leaned down, and picked up the Lieutenant from the ground by his arms as well. Lifted him up and dropped him on the tailgate and rolls him into the bed of the truck, stepped back, and lifted up and shut the tailgate of the truck, turns to me and said, ‘In the truck!’

“Gavin walks over to the cop car and drives the car way out into the field. A half-hour or hour goes by. I hear scuffling. I look over and see Gavin is almost back to the truck. A couple more minutes, he opens the door, jumps in, and starts it up. We pull off, drove for a few hours.

***

Surprisingly; we drove back to the house.

"Gavin and I pull up to the barn and get out the truck. He walked around to the back of the truck. I open the tailgate as Gavin open the barn doors. He walked back to me and the truck, reached in, and drags both the cops out of the bed of the truck, dropping them onto the ground. He dragged the cops into the barn, through the floor door, down the steps, and down the hall into the room. He shoves the Sargent into the little holding room. Gavin walks back over to the Lieutenant, drags him up into the chair. Gavin and I took turns torturing him.

"I brought this triangle thing over to Gavin. He latched the chain hook on to the angled metal, walked to the column. He tugged on the chain, stringing up the cop, and begins torturing him again. While he was having his fun, I walked to the tool table and pulled out a fillet knife, turned back around, and walked over to Marriessa, who is still strapped to the rack table. I be- gan to butcher Marriessa's body. She didn't scream for long, She was already half dead before I started. Gavin stops torturing the Lieutenant. He walks over to me, grabs a chunk of Marriessa's thigh, and cooks it on the mini barbecue, as I continue cutting the muscles off her body.

"When her thigh was finished, he walked over to me. I stopped butchering Marriessa, and we ate. Then he lifted me up and leaned me back over her cut up body and fucked me, forcing me in many different positions, as I got covered in her blood, rolling around in her body parts. When we finished screwing, we went up to the house, showered, and slept.

***

"For the next month, we went out once a week, torturing, slaughtering, and murdering families, framing the Sargent for all the murders Gavin and I committed.

***

"A couple weeks went by. I gave birth to our son. We named him Ayden. He was seven pounds, six ounces. A few months lat- er, Gavin was getting antsy, our son now four months old. Gavin wanted to teach another lesson, as he called it. I told him I do not want to, and he beat the hell out of me. Next thing I know,

***

"I'm lying in the dirt, wrapped in plastic, and you cops are everywhere.

***

"I must've passed out. As I looked around, I noticed I was in the hospital and now I'm here with y'all, which means my son is with his father."

The Sheriff yelled out to one of the other cops. 'Someone wanna get her a cup of coffee.'

"Then he sat in the chair across from me, quietly for hours. What seemed like hours. The small-town cops come back into the shop, with no Gavin and no Ayden. The Sheriff stood up, turned his back to me, and opened the door. There is some greasy redneck-looking guy in the window.

"Sheriff asked, 'Where are they?'

"All of the cops just had a confused, daunting look on their face. I stood up from the chair, leaned over the table, pulled out the Sheriff's gun from the holster. Backed away from the table, putting the tip of the barrel to the right side of my head,'He doesn't want me! I'm not worthy.'

‘As tears streamed from her eyes, Callisto said, ‘Ayden, I love you.’ After a brief moment, she went on to say, ‘I can’t live without, I won’t live without, I, I’m sorry.’

“Before I could say a word, the Sheriff turned back around to see what it is she was saying. She pulled the trigger. Her brains blew out of the left side of her head, all over the wall, floor and table.

Sheriff yells, ‘NO!’

“As her body dropped to the floor. The sheriff stepped forward against the corner of the table and dropped to his knees, staring at Callisto’s lifeless body.

“He said, ‘Somebody, Get the, Get the Judge on the phone.’ Then yells, ‘Find them. Find the boy, and that Fuckin Gavin!’”

www.ingramcontent.com/pod-product-compliance
Lightning Source LLC
Chambersburg PA
CBHW070627310726
48982CB00001B/193

* 9 7 8 0 9 9 8 6 7 1 5 0 5 *